MW01118647

Unreal
and
Surreal

Jo-Jo Tabayoyong Murphy

Gina!
Thank you for
helping me distinguish
between the levels
of energy. I am
grateful.
Love,
Jo-Jo

Also by Jo-Jo Tabayoyong Murphy

American Stew on Rice
Your Lunch Smells Funny
Bless This Bite

DEDICATION

For my parents, Wesley and Evangeline Tabayoyong,
who introduced me to the magic in books and libraries.

CONTENTS

ACKNOWLEDGMENTS

I was born with a vivid, Technicolor imagination.
Sometimes that creative streak got me into trouble.
I did not always preface a story by saying whether it was true.
When someone asked a question, I often had a burst of
inspiration that sounded much better than reality. Let me take
this opportunity to apologize to my siblings and cousins for
sometimes
shoving them into a surreal world without warning.

For example, I told them about the miniature people inside
our television and my special twist that could take heads
on and off their necks.
I half-believed what I told them.

Many thanks to my pals at the Writing Factory for being my
attentive peers. Your suggestions and comments have
helped shape my writing pieces.

Several relatives and friends look at my work
in its early stages.
I appreciate their candor, skill, and time.

As always, I am lucky to have my husband Steve's input.
He listens as I read aloud my finished work,
then lets me know his honest opinion.
In our marriage, we balance truth with kindness.

FAIR TRADE

He had been sitting down to dinner when he heard it.

"Tap tap tap taaaaaaap."

There it was! The damned snippet had been haunting him. Whenever he sat at the piano to elaborate on it, nothing else came. He wanted to do more with this tantalizing concept, but he was disturbed by the sounds of clanking in the kitchen, his own foot tapping the wooden floor, and a bird singing outside the window. Even the steady beating of his own impatient heart distracted him. He could not seem to concentrate long enough to complete a piece of any length.

After working diligently every day, he always took himself outdoors for a walk. Some of these jaunts took hours. The leafy ground absorbed sounds that usually annoyed him. On these afternoons, he could devise ways of dealing with elusive chord progressions. Lilting songs would inspire him as he hiked. He always went alone. There were altogether too many people around these days. Thankfully, very few ventured into the forest on weekdays. He could wander freely.

His hearing loss had been gradual at first. His maid told others the master had developed selective hearing. He could not hear her knock at his studio door, but he always knew when she dropped a cup in the house!

As this was happening, he noticed that one particular musical phrase insinuated its way into his brain every day. There were even nights when it would form a persistent background for his dreams. Four notes, three short and one long, seemed to cycle endlessly.

He sat at the piano to work on commissioned pieces. This new sonata was due for his patron in a few weeks. He needed to write the Adagio movement, but he could not focus. That cloying phrase - completely inappropriate for a slow melody - would not leave him in peace!

The torture went on for more than a month.

This afternoon, he had become extremely agitated. That fool servant had broken yet another precious piece of his family's china. Some sort of vendor had stood outside on the street and caterwauled about his wares until hot tea was poured from the second-floor window. Too bad the wind had carried the scalding stream away from the idiot's head!

He chose to take his walk early today.

The demonic tune had filled his head as soon as he left the paved road. Was there no solace anywhere?

He had begun to wonder whether his sanity was at risk. How could he be losing a sense of hearing if this rhythmic quartet of notes could be so sharp and clear?

An old prayer his nanny had taught him came to mind. He was cynical. Though he wrote many religious works, he had begun to doubt the omniscient God of his nursery days. If only to shut out the maddening bits, he began to pray, "Lord God, if you are able to hear me, please spare me from these hellish notes! If I am to use them, give me clarity and direction. If they come from the Devil himself, send your angels down to douse my ears so that I may not hear his siren call."

He repeated the prayer like a rosary. It soothed him as he made his way into darker parts of the familiar woods. His breathing slowed, his pulse slowed, and he could feel a respite that his life had lacked for many months.

That is when he heard the firm, powerful voice assail him. "Are you certain that this is what you want? Do you know what you are asking?"

If he had not been a man in such exquisite control of his body, he might have fallen to the ground. "Lord, is it truly you?"

"Yes, my son. I will grant you this petition, but I must be sure that you understand what will be required of you in return."

"I did not think a loving God would ask for a sacrifice if a request were made sincerely and unselfishly."

"*I* decide the rules here. Are you willing?"

"What will happen?"

"I will assist your natural talents and skills by presenting you with certain melodies. It will be up to you to refine those until they form meaningful pieces of art."

"Doesn't sound sacrificial."

"You asked for the distractions to be removed. How did you think that would happen?"

"You are God. I have no idea, though I suspect my faulty ears may come into play."

"I will draw you closer to my world in such a way that you can no longer sense secular noises. All you will hear will be celestial."

"No more screaming fishmongers? No more clattering brooms? No more off-key whistling from my staff? Lord, this is truly the answer I have sought."

"Welcome, my son, to the higher realm of sound. Let us create music that will resonate for centuries."

"Thy will be done."

He ran back home. A wagon clattered near him. Thankfully, the vibration was loud enough to warn him because he never heard a whisper. He stomped up the stairs to his studio, completely oblivious to the question Cook posed regarding supper. He marched purposefully to the piano bench and sat down to compose.

That was when the reality of this new situation flooded his brain. He would never again hear his music performed! He could sit at a piano and write notes, but he would not be able to listen for pleasing harmonies or complex counterpoint. This would be the punishment of a damned soul. He began to sob.

Quietly, insistently, and gradually getting louder, he heard that familiar phrase come to him. From force of habit, he wrote down the notes. He formed chords with his hands on the keys, knowing he would not hear the actual piano. He was astounded to find that he could still imagine how they would sound. The piano had become a part of his body.

He took a deep shuddering breath, wiped the salty sting of horror from his eyes, and began doing his life's work.

RESTING PLACE

"Pack your two favorite small toys, one book, and three changes of clothes. Everything must fit into this bag. We must be ready by dinner time tonight. Do you understand?"

"Yes, Mom. Are you sure I can't take my bigger stuff? I don't need that many clothes. I would rather have three books than one more pair of pants."

"We are not negotiating. Please go and get this done right away."

"Okay, Dad. What will happen to all our stuff after we go?"

"That's not our worry. We would rather have you than anything else we keep in this shelter."

I remember that conversation so well. I could not understand what was happening. One morning, we got the announcement that transports would take us to the new settlement. We barely had time to wipe the sleep out of our eyes before my parents started taking bags out of the storage area.

This had happened once before. That first time, I had been too young to remember any of it. My older siblings told me how we had rushed out of our big, comfortable home with almost no warning. Some of our neighbors had disregarded the sirens. We never saw them again.

Now, everyone pays attention.

Our new living space is nice. My dearest friend lives beside us. We play after study time is finished. I like our common areas because we can sometimes see shimmers of light, plants, and birds overhead. Last time, we cowered in darkness. We were not allowed to turn on any illumination during waking hours. It was hard to run and jump with my mates. We learned games that used sounds and rhythms. We only had room to sleep, eat, and sit upright.

I hope we stay here for a while.

The other day, I caught my mom wiping away tears from her cheeks. She was ashamed when she saw me. I hardly ever hear her complain. She has never looked discouraged. My dad makes us feel better. He sings as he does chores. My family likes to give hugs and kisses. I think that may be why my friend likes our quarters so much. Next door, the grown-ups scold, yell at each other, and frown a lot.

My parents say that some of our people had not wanted to leave their homesteads. They had not believed there was any danger. They felt betrayed by our leaders. Even though we saw pictures and films of the destruction later on, they were still dissatisfied and restless.

Mom quietly tells us to be kind to the grumpy ones. Some of them do not have anyone to give them cuddles.

We kids feel lucky to be able to share our stuff. I have

memorized all of our books, so I make up my own. I hope I will be able to take them with me if we have to move again. If not, I will share old ones with my buddies. Some of them have nothing to amuse them during play time.

Once in a while, all of us gather in the central space. We watch movies, performances, and lectures there. Those who are musicians or artists are allowed to have some of their instruments and tools carried in the transports. Our leaders insist that we need distractions and entertainment to keep us happy. They are right!

As the light begins to fade, I can peek outside and see the faint glow of the sky. If it is a very clear night, I lay on my back to count the first few stars. One looks kind of pink. Mom and Dad told us that it is our old home. I cannot remember what it was like to live way up there. Did I ever look up and see this place? Did I have a feeling that I would one day see it up close?

At our last concert, we heard a song about leaving what is familiar. The older folks in our group cried a bit. I have no clear memories of our first escape, but I do know what it is like to pull things off shelves in a hurry.

Mom says that home is wherever the six of us sleep peacefully. If we think of it that way, we do not have to weep about changing addresses.

I have celebrated ten birthdays since my feet were planted on that faraway star. Each time I blow out the candles, I wish for a region that has lots of open areas. I want to have an unlimited field where I can stretch my legs, watch the lights sparkle and dim, and run until I am breathless. I hope my family gets assigned to a place we never have to surrender again.

Until then, we keep our bags in easy reach. We do not get attached to anything except each other. We sing to remind us of where we once were. We bloom inside, where walls need not protect us.

Jo-Jo Tabayoyong Murphy

BREAKING, BRAVING, BLAZING

I looked ahead.

My spirit hiccupped.

I moved shyly and did not fall.

I stood firm.

I would go until my essence dissolved.

I shook, but the earth was constant.

I found access despite sheer cliffs.

I hoisted up others who had stumbled.

Now, we nudge each other on.

We laugh when breathing is too taxing.

We save our words when a glance is enough.

We have a rhythm that carries us further with less toil.

We pause and know that we can continue.

We are where, and when, we are meant to be.

We are always arriving.

ROMAN SANDALS

Marching through the dust,
Building edifices that defend the empire.
Hoisting spear, shield, and sword;
Guarding our conquered lands as though we were born there.

My life is directed by a Caesar
Who does not know my name.
He cares not whether I have a wife or babies or aging parents.
I serve and must surrender my life upon command.
As the shadow of Rome darkens more of the world,
I walk farther and farther away from home.

One day, I will see my village shining on a hot summer day.
My thirst will be slaked by the pure waters of a simple well.
Fruit grown in my mother's garden will seem like a feast.
The last thing I will see as I close my eyes will be the face of
my beloved in repose.
My sons will ride upon my shoulders as we walk to the
market.
The tales I tell of my centurion life will be brief.
I dare not speak of the horrors lest they haunt their dreams as
they do mine.

Today I look upon the people of a foreign soil
And recognize that they are much like me.
I weep during starry nights as I stand watch.
My youthful strength is spent on causing pain.
Will I ever become an old, stumbling man?
Or will my final breaths in this world be taken
Before I have had a chance to remove these
Thick leather sandals and bathe my feet
in the stream beside my home?

ANTIDOTE

It was dark, a headache was consuming all my attention, and I just wanted some relief. I reached beside my bed and grabbed a medicine container out of my purse. I didn't want to wake my husband, so I popped the pills without water. This is a skill I developed after taking birth control tablets for years. When you want to stay childless, you take that pill at the same time every day, without fail and without water, if necessary.

It was vitally important that I get a decent night's sleep. I had to face an intimidating situation in the morning. My biggest fan/stalker, a vicious woman named Hester Sneed was going to be at the airport. She had been following me around from city to city. This trip to London was the last leg of my tour. I knew that I could give a huge final concert, then disappear for a few months of complete privacy and rest. I just had to sneak past Hester and her obtrusive camera to get to the waiting limo. Once Security put me in that car, I would be safe.

I had a restraining order against Hester, but it didn't seem to faze her. She felt that airports, theaters, and even city parks were in the public domain. She could appear anywhere, at any time, unless I managed to surround myself with burly bodyguards or eat Italian food. Odd, but true. She could not abide the scent of garlic. Perhaps she was part vampire? I could feel at ease in a pizza joint, most Asian food places, and even the occasional hot dog cart, if the scent of the stinkin' rose was redolent.

Today, I had succumbed to temptation and had a huge platter of spaghetti á la carbonara. I was sensitive to bacon, but it was so delicious here in Boston. My favorite restaurant kept its doors open extra late so that I could eat there after my performances. My entourage was happy, too. We all enjoyed dining at Luva Dis Food.

That's why I was suffering at 2 a.m. My intake of all those preservatives and sulfates had brought on a raging migraine. If I caught it early, I could avoid the vomiting and nausea that were the wily partners of these headaches. I didn't want to be using the airsick bag before the plane got off the runway!

Hopefully, Hester was also feeling under the weather after she caught a whiff of Chef Antonio's specialties! I had asked the busboys to leave as many windows open as possible. I had wanted all those powerful odors to fill the streets surrounding us.

I closed my eyes and tried to catch a few hours of sleep. The medicine seemed to be working. At least I was feeling more drowsy and tired now.

We woke up the next day before the alarm went off. I think we were thrilled to be seeing the end of the grueling five-month tour.

My hubby let me go to the bathroom first. He tried to catch a few more precious moments of sleep. I went quietly to the hotel's spacious facilities and didn't turn on the big overhead lights. I knew that my eyes were still getting accustomed to being open. It was 4 a.m. and there was not much ambient light in the room. I finished my business and went to wake my patient life partner.

He groaned as I tapped his shoulder. As he sat up, he started to say good morning, then recoiled in horror! "Wh-what happened to your face?!"

"Nice. Is that any way to greet your honey?"

"Really. Have you seen yourself in the mirror yet?"

"No. I didn't want to see bright lights for at least a few more minutes. Why? You're not kidding, are you?"

He walked me over to the dresser and stood behind me as I got a glimpse of myself.

I screamed. It was enough to send my security guards rushing to the door. They thought Hester had climbed up the side of the four-story boutique hotel.

My cheeks were twice their normal size. My eyes were so puffy, it looked as though I'd been repeatedly beaten by big-fisted thugs. Even my ears were swollen. I resembled an ogre. My own mother wouldn't have recognized me.

"Are you allergic to your favorite spaghetti now?"

"Of course not! I just had that dish about three weeks ago. Chef Antonio sent me some when I was in New York.

Nothing happened to me that time. This is horrible."

"Are you using some other make-up or shampoo?"

"Let me think. Wait, hand me that medicine on the nightstand!"

"The only thing here is a bottle of aspirin."

I shrieked again. Luckily, my guards were already in the room. I am horribly allergic to aspirin. I hadn't taken it since I was about three years old. Back then, my whole body had gotten red, itchy, and distended. I looked like a big, rosy Michelin gal. I had carefully avoided it ever since. Last night, I had been so desperate for my pain to stop that I'd gulped down whatever I'd found in my purse. I forgot that I was carrying Bayer for one of my band members.

The hotel doctor gave me some Benadryl and a stronger antihistamine in case that didn't work. I felt okay after taking it. That was the good news. The bad news was that I would probably have a pumpkin head for a few more hours.

On the plus side, Hester did not recognize the woman in the bandana-wrapped hair who left our hotel in the bright sunshine. I wore stiletto heels and some over-sized sunglasses to complete the look. I felt free and completely invisible. When I arrived in London, the *Daily Mail* commented that Lady Leigh was looking very well-rested and glamorous.

I may use that aspirin trick again.

CHESHIRE CASHIER

"47 bottles of beer on the wall .... "

Where was the next exit? I knew there were vast gaps between inhabited areas of New Mexico, but I was not prepared to have that wall be cleared of and restocked with ale three times in a row. I considered my options: popping in another mind-numbing Caillou DVD, keeping our kids from squabbling over the "I Spy" game when there were few landmarks, or fielding questions about our non-imminent arrival at the motel where I prayed to God there would be a clean swimming pool.

I heaved a mental sigh of exasperation. I cursed the field trip that had taught them this loathsome tune.

"Daddy! There's a sign for McDonald's!" The two oldest offspring began squirming and squealing. Our toddler started to scream, too. My wife and I shared a quick look. Normally, we avoided dining under those Golden Arches, but on this trip, the kids had enjoyed the indoor playgrounds often enough to recognize the signs.

I sped up.

We barely got their sandals on before they wanted to tear into the restaurant. Luckily, there was only one other car in the parking lot and it had been there a while, judging by the thick layer of dust on its surface.

My nifty partner took the bigger heirs to the play area while I wheeled our youngest over to place our orders. The baby fussed until the perky teen grinned at him. The transformation was immediate. The tiny terror sat still. I was stunned. Then, those bright blue eyes and sparkling teeth were pointed at me. I suddenly understood.

Imagine an Osmond and Zoë De Chanel combining their most salient features. Then, add the charisma of the Pied Piper.

This young lad would one day be President of these United States or the most successful snake oil salesman ever known!

I ordered three Happy Meals, two apple pies, two shakes, three Big Macs, a salad, and large fries. Did I mention my wife and I normally feed our brood organic veggies? Do you now understand the power of this high school boy's grin?

He helped me carry our bounty over to the picnic table my wife had secured for us. Her eyes snapped open when she saw what I had decided to feed our precious children. I shook my head so that she would save her ranting for later.

Mr. Blue Sky flashed her his winning sunshiny smile and the lecture disappeared in a poof of fryer smoke. I snorted because she looked as smitten as I had felt.
"Do you need anything else, folks?"

"No, you have taken good care of us," gushed the mother of my brood. When the paper-hatted charmer graced her with an appreciative full-grill smile, she actually blushed! I had never seen her act like a giddy Beatles fan before.

Who was this Adonis? Was he a wizard of fast food salesmanship? Would we leave with our cholesterol levels elevated and our hippy ideals shattered?

We could not coax our two wild ones out of the treehouse tunnels.

I turned as he began to walk away. As if he anticipated my thoughts, he moved toward the slide and called out to them. "If you eat most of your chicken nuggets and fruit, your mom and dad will show you the toys I put in your bags!"

My oldest was born in New Jersey. She trusts no one. She skedaddled out of the plastic tubing as though dragons pursued her.

My number two daughter hates to be pulled away from playing. She followed her sister so closely that the two of them rode down the slide together!

I wanted to offer this guy a position as caregiver, effective immediately. I was willing to pay more than double the minimum wage that Ronald McDonald put in his measly paycheck. My wife looked as though she might volunteer as a surrogate for his spawn.

When he walked back to the counter, it was as though the sun had set. My children were subdued as they slowly ate a few bites of their processed fare.

We all waved sad good-byes as he held open the door.

What is the penalty for kidnapping?

I wish I had thought to snap a photo. We could have created posters and paid three college tuitions with the profits.

REFLECTIONS

Floating pink top
Clingy denim short shorts
Metallic sandals with serious heels
And a proud bearing
That carried her across the street
As though mignons were bearing her
On a golden litter.

The forgettable male,
Who followed her with
A possessive hand on the small of her back,
Seemed to need that contact
To feel attached.
She may as well have been alone.
There were no glances exchanged.

She strode confidently
Her arms swinging in graceful arcs,
Eyes focused forward,
No hesitation in her walk.
He glanced around furtively
Plucking at her sleeve or
Brushing hair from his face.

I watched them move
Wondering about their connection.
As they reached the sidewalk,
He swatted her backside
Suddenly, and with more force than affection.
Her head jerked momentarily,
But she barely missed a step.

Did I imagine tears welling in her eyes?
She kept going silently.
He snorted and checked to see
Whether other uncouth witnesses
Appreciated his boorish act.
They blended into the crowd
And I never saw them again.

A cat can look at a king,
Or so I have heard.
A man's reach should exceed his grasp,
Or is it the other way around?
Shall this woman grope beneath her level
Just to have the company she craves?
Or did that slap awaken her from a stupor?

I searched the grounds to find them,
But never caught their shadows.
Did I imagine this occurrence
As I watched strangers mill about?

Or was I treated to a rare insight
As I caught my reflection in a store window,
Storming away from a partner
Whose hands only brought me pain?

JUST A SONG BEFORE I GO

He had never touched a girl's waist before. He hoped he would not look like a buffoon. He was glad the lights were dimmed to conserve energy. There was a war on, after all.

Georgie was normally quiet and liked to stand behind the other guys on a dance floor. Tonight was special. Tomorrow, his unit was getting on a train and heading to New York. This could be his last party at home. He had never been more than a night's drive away from here.

The young men he had known all his life looked awkward. Six of them had enlisted together. Three of them had passed the physical. Two were packed and ready to ship out. The rest were disappointed, but some had mentioned that they were hoping to try again. Maybe other branches of the military would not be so picky?

He hadn't come here to be with the boys. There was only one person he wanted to see. Emily was the prettiest girl he'd ever known. He'd been sweet on her since the third grade. He had never been brave enough to have a long conversation with her, let alone ask her to dance. If he was about to cross a wide, churning ocean to fight the enemy, surely he could get up the gumption to walk up to some female at a party. He knew that Emily had just gotten a special necklace for her 18th birthday. It had belonged to her mother. She was wearing it tonight. Georgie had begged his uncle's band to play the nation's most popular song as the first number.

The introductory notes of "String of Pearls" got everyone excited. He could hear whispers and muffled chuckling coming from the coat room. That was where the girls gathered before the event started. He sure hoped Emily would come out of there soon or he would miss his chance.

There she was!

He walked quickly over to her before he lost his nerve. "Excuse me, Emily, would you care to dance?"

She blushed and looked over her shoulder, as if she thought he might be talking to someone else. "Hi, Georgie. Sure, that would be nice."

He lightly took her hand. Gosh, it was tiny! They moved to the middle of the crowd. He tried hard to keep the beat of the song. His feet were not accustomed to wearing such slippery dress shoes.

Emily had an effortless grace. She let him lead, though he could feel her guidance when he lost the rhythm. She kept them going so that they didn't bump into any other couples. When he stumbled, she gave him a look of understanding. His heart almost exploded with gratitude.

26

"Those pearls sure are special. They look good with your, um, earrings," Georgie stammered. "Hey, they're the same color as your necklace!"

"Thank you, Georgie. They were made to match. My grandmother gave me the earrings and my mom handed down her necklace. It's a family tradition."

"Well, that sure is a swell way of doing things."

"I think so, too. All three of us cried a little as they gave them to me." She blushed again. "I guess we all love this jewelry. We've been looking forward to this for a long time."

Changing the subject, she asked, "How do you feel about going on this long voyage?"

As if the music heard her, they could hear "Sentimental Journey" start playing.

"Would you like to keep dancing?"

Emily gave him a long look and nodded.

Georgie thought this might just be the happiest moment of his whole life.

From the stage, his uncle watched his favorite nephew swaying with his best girl. He motioned to his band members to repeat the song. Why not draw out the magic for this young couple? Life would change soon enough.

CHASING CRIMSON

She took a slow, calming breath and pushed open the lab door. It was her first night on the job as a phlebotomist. She hoped she did not look at all like a 700-year-old to her patients.

"Good evening, Nurse Scarlett. Welcome to the Starlight Free Clinic. I look forward to working with you."

"Thank you, Dr. Russett. I have heard lots of compliments about your practice. I hope to be an asset."

After a quick tour of the small space, Scarlett was shown to her work area and began to make herself familiar with all her equipment. The physician smiled and went into his own office. He had chosen this young woman himself. Her decades as a lab tech would make her very useful. This was a poor community. They had had more business than they could handle during the busy summer months.

Despite the almost shabby appearance of the outer areas, the labs and treatment rooms were tidy, clean, and well-appointed. Their staff was chosen carefully for their calm under pressure, bedside manner, and good humor. This neighborhood was fortunate that such a place existed.

Original artwork decorated the brightly colored walls. She peered closely at the signature. It was a name she knew. It surprised her that the painting was not a reproduction or a pop art poster.

There was a cushy chair for her under a modern lamp, designed to make a person feel at home. It had a warmth that was not typical for a healthcare provider's office. It reminded her of doctors' rooms from the early days of the 20th century, if one did not look too closely at the state-of-the-art machinery.

She heard a soft knock at the door. "Come in!"

A shy young woman walked inside, accompanied by a sniffling little boy. "Hello, nurse. My name is Rose. Stop crying now, Junior. You know you are too big for boohooing."

"My name is Miss Scarlett. Have a seat right here, my friend. Is this your mom? She can be next to you. I have an extra chair. What's your name?"

He looked at her and started sobbing. His mom looked embarrassed and hugged him. He put his head on her shoulder and would not look at Scarlett.

"Oh, my. It must be hard to be out of bed at this hour. Have you ever been awake this late before?"

The question startled him. He shook his head. "My bedtime is at 7 o'clock. I never go out of the house after Mommy tucks me in."

"How does it feel to be seeing all the street lights on? I think it looks like fairy land!"

"I saw the bridge when we came here. It has big white bulbs all over the top. I like them."

Rose smiled at her. Scarlett asked him whether he could sit by himself now. He looked at the nurse's kind face and scooted over on the examining table. Scarlett gave an inward sigh of relief.

"Let me explain what I am going to do for you. May I call you Junior?"

"My name is Rolf, just like my daddy!"

"Okay, Rolf. I see from this piece of paper that you are not feeling well. The doctor needs to find out what is going on. If he figures out which germs are making you sick, he can help you get better. Did he ask you some questions?"

Rolf gave a small nod. His mother explained that he had been running a very high temperature for several days. Over-the-counter drugs briefly helped it lessen, but were no longer doing any good.

"There is a flu bug that has been spreading around the city this week. Have you had friends who missed school?" Another nod came. "We have to find out whether you have that sickness. I have to give the doctor some clues. My job is to take a little bit of blood from your arm so that he can check for those germs."

Whimpers started again. "It is going to hurt!"

"Yes, you will feel a little pinch at first. I have been doing this a long time. Some people do not feel anything more than a mosquito bite. Have you gotten any of those this summer?"

Rose teased, "We went to the park last week. Junior played outside so long that his legs had more bites than smooth spots!" This made the little boy grin.

"Rolf, did you slap at any of those biters?"

"I smacked a few of them!"

"Well, if you can take that kind of slap without falling over, then this will be an easy thing for you."

He took a breath and said, "You can take my blood, but I don't have to watch, do I?"

"Nope! Your mom can hold you in her lap while I do it. Will that make you feel better?"

He glanced at his mom and she ruffled his hair. He was ready.

Scarlett used quick, efficient movements and got the job done in just a few seconds. Her patient was quiet and still. His mom hummed a little tune, closing her own eyes while the blood filled two vials. Seeing that they weren't watching, she deftly added a third small vial to the regimen. When it was finished, Scarlett let him pick out an Iron Man Band-Aid.

"You have been one of my bravest patients, Rolf! Thank you."

"That was not so bad after all. You did not make me cry

when you used the needle." He gave her a big hug.

They shook hands and Rose wiped a tear from her eye. "You have been wonderful. I am indebted to you, nurse."

"I hope you feel well soon, Rolf. Rose, I hope you can sleep as soon as you get back home. We should have the results of the blood test by the morning. The doctor will prescribe something for the fever."

When they left, Scarlett sank into the reclining chair. It was good to be back at work, doing what she enjoyed. She had been on the move for several weeks. She hoped that this would be a resting place for some time.

She transferred one of the vials to a separate cooler. That would be her 2 a.m. snack.

A PICTURE PAINTS A THOUSAND BIRDS

As a student teacher, I helped a group of teenagers learn how to write fiction. They taught me how to shift my inner clock to the rhythms of Rio. When I left Brazil, these students gave me a painting of the rainforest. The birds looked so colorful and vibrant, they could have launched themselves into my classroom. I cried when the kids presented me with such a special good-bye gift.

The memento has a place of honor in my spare bedroom. I tried hanging it above my desk, but it made me too homesick. I put it in a spot that I do not see very often.

Yesterday, my cousin and her new husband came to visit me. Instead of offering my guest room, I gave them my own bedroom. It has a bigger mattress.

We stayed up until almost dawn, drinking wine and catching up on family news. We agreed to sleep until we all felt rested. I lurched down the hall and fell into bed.

The sun hits that part of the house at a weird angle. I forgot to draw the curtains all the way, so I was awakened by a bright shaft of light. It illuminated the artwork. I lay in bed and took a good look at the brilliant brush strokes for the first time in months.

What was that? I rubbed my eyes and sat up straighter. How much wine had I consumed last night?

The birds seemed to turn their heads to follow my movements. I had better buy a higher quality hooch for the relatives. I hoped they were not suffering monstrous hangovers.

I realized that my head didn't ache, my body was rested, and I could see perfectly.

Why did the two birds now have their wings neatly folded? I recalled that the one on the left had been painted with its wings outstretched. I gave a low, breathy whistle.

Hang on! Both birds were startled into flying. They disappeared into the back of the scene and I was left with a simple landscape.

"Whoa! What is going on?"

Sandy came running into my room. "Are you okay?"

"Take a look at that picture. Does it look odd to you?"

She walked over to the wall and gave the painting a quick glance. "No, this looks fine. I never saw it before, but it looks intact. Why? Has it been damaged? What made you yell?"

I shook my head sharply. I bounced out of the covers and took the painting off the wall. There was no sign of damage. I even turned it over as I considered the possibility that the birds had flown out of the back. I sheepishly realized what I was doing and put it back on its hook.

"You will never believe what I just saw. I must be feeling a buzz from our party last night. I thought I watched two parrots leave this scene. Crazy, right?"

Sandy gave me a quick hug. "Let's have some coffee. We could both use a little boost after a short night. I'll get it started. Go on and clean up a little. Maybe if you wash your face, you'll feel more level-headed?"

I agreed. Had I been hallucinating?

After I splashed cold water on my eyes and gave my teeth a good scrub, I went back to the room for my robe. It was chilly at that hour.

I glanced at the wall and jumped backwards. One of the birds had come back!

That's it. No more bargain wine for this gal.

I poked my head into the kitchen and quietly asked Sandy to come over to my room. She put the coffee mugs down and joined me.

"Are you feeling dizzy? May I get you something?"

"Look at the painting again, cuz. Please tell me I am not off my rocker."

She gave me a wry smile and turned her back to me. She whirled around. "What on earth? That bird wasn't there ten minutes ago!"

I sat down on the bed. She plopped down beside me. We giggled nervously.

"Did you bake something extra in those brownies? We had better drink a lot of caffeine today. Lex will get a good howl out of this when he wakes up."

"Why am I going to be amused? Are you two doing something goofy?" Lex wandered in. "I heard some noises coming from back here and could not believe you had gotten out of bed so early."

I gave Sandy a look we had used as kids. It meant, "Keep this between us."

"Lex, I'm sorry we woke you. I had a nightmare and my scream scared Sandy."

"You ladies had too much boxed wine and too little food. No wonder you had disturbing thoughts!"

I shooed them out of the room and told them to go back to bed. Sandy gave my hand a lingering squeeze as she left. We both gazed at the painting. No changes since the last time.

They shut the door behind them. I decided to read for a while. I was much too agitated to go back to sleep. I closed my curtains firmly.

After fifteen minutes of a dull novel, I felt drowsy. I didn't turn my head toward the framed art as I turned off the lamp. No need to frighten myself any more.

We all slept for another few hours. By the time I got out of my pajamas and into some jeans, I felt like a new woman. I bravely faced my fears and the wretched painting.

It looked exactly as it had when my class lovingly handed it to me. There were two parrots, one about to fly and one sitting contentedly on the tree.

I began another low whistle, then thought better of it. I whipped open all the curtains and walked toward the door. I must have only imagined that I heard the soft rustle of wings.

HOARSE CODE

There were no more words. Ideas were expressed using abbreviations, shortened grunts, hand signals, and pictures. The shift had come slowly at first. People said things such as, "Got it!" when they understood. Approval was met with "Cool!" Then, typing became more prevalent than handwriting.

We did not grasp that complete sentences were being phased out. At church services, we gave each other greetings during worship by holding up one hand and making a V sign with two fingers. This was how we said, "Peace be with you." It was short, sweet, and easy. The pastor never criticized this practice. She was too busy trying to tell us about the word of God using a projection screen and PowerPoint presentations. Boilerplate dogma became the norm. Religious services were reduced to YouTube videos. One no longer had to wake up early on Sunday morning, go to temple on Friday at sunset, or bow toward Mecca. All that was required was an Internet connection.

Babies babbled and were not corrected. The spoken word consisted of snickers, tsk tsk tsk, uh-huh, unh-unh, and nah.

Sales of cough drops, mouthwash, and microphones

dwindled. We opened our mouths only to eat, drink, or yawn with boredom.

One fine day, Rip was awakened from a coma. This young man had been in a state of non-communication for twenty-five years. After being hit by a car, his family had helped him stay safe, kept him hydrated and nourished, and watched over him.

Once his eyes were opened, he startled his sister by asking, "What day is this?"

She had not heard him – or many others, speak a word since the previous century. She dropped her electronic device and jumped to her feet!

She could not answer him verbally, so she picked up her tablet and showed him the date at the top of her screen. He looked at her curiously and read that it was over two decades since he had been aware of anything.

"Why can't you answer me? Are you sick? Have you lost your voice?"

She merely shook her head and said, "Nah."

Mystified, he tried to sit up. She raised the head of his hospital bed and pressed the call button for his nurse.

A small man in colorful scrubs appeared at the doorway. He gasped and walked over to the patient. Checking vital signs and monitor readings, his eyes widened and he began efficiently tallying indicators on a computer screen.

Rip spoke softly, so as not to surprise the nurse. "Would you please tell me what happened? Why am I in the hospital?"

The nurse glanced at him and shrugged. He pointed to the computer screen, then to his watch. He seemed unconcerned by Rip's growing frustration.

Rip looked at his silent sister and motioned her closer. "Can you tell me how more than two decades disappeared?"

She looked nervous and gave the nurse a meaningful look. The two of them sighed and she pressed the call button once more.

Several other white-coated staff people gathered in the room, no one making a sound. Rip began raising his voice, repeating his question, and waving his hands in their faces excitedly. The care providers began backing away from the bed, shaking their heads and grunting.

"Unh-unh."

One looked triumphant and raised his hand in the Peace gesture.

Rip was horrified. Did that mute fool think that was enough to explain away the disappearance of one's youth?

In the corner of his hospital room, a wrinkled old woman rose from her chair. She shuffled over to the bed and took Rip's hand.

In a modulated, beautiful voice she began talking to her grandson. "Rip, you were in a terrible car accident. You were jogging down the road when someone lost control of their vehicle. We thought we had lost you, but that fighting spirit kept your heart beating and brain working. You've been unconscious all these years. We have never given up hope. Thank God you have come back to us!"

"Granny, why is no one else speaking to me? Are they afraid? Am I dreaming or dead?"

"My darling boy, you have slept through some changes that have been made in the world. People no longer communicate with each other in ways that you knew. In fact, I haven't used my own voice in public for quite some time. Our family humors me. They let me talk, but no one responds verbally. They send me electronic messages. I have had to adjust. Did you ever think you would see me using a computer?"

Rip sank back in his bed with relief. He wasn't in Hell. He was in limbo. He would have to learn to use the inventions of the past few years in order to make himself understood.

Good thing his thumbs had not been amputated during the accident.

MOOD INDIGO

Smuggled pens passed from hand to hand. Small notes were folded into napkins, tucked under tea cups, and buried under rose bushes. Voting took place surreptitiously. We were sworn to the utmost secrecy. Discovery of our actions would be ruinous.

She ascends today!

We know her name now.

It is written in code on leaves added to floral arrangements. We see the signs everywhere, but only because we are aware of them.

Smiles of elation are smothered. If we cheer, it must be done under cover of darkness or heavy shawls. The auspicious day has arrived!

The Indigo Quill is an honor given to females who have the courage and audacity to push for an education, no matter what obstacles they have overcome.

This year's recipient had disguised herself as a boy, found ways to access Internet classes, and defied local laws to learn her lessons. We marveled at her bravery and persistence. She had managed to earn a high school diploma in an area where girls could barely scratch symbols in sand.

Our corps had formed when education was denied to anyone with that double X chromosome pattern. It had been decreed that limited resources would not be wasted on bodies that were smaller, frailer, and prone to monthly limitations.

The shock had been widespread and vocal - at least in the beginning. When we saw how swiftly and horribly detractors had been punished, the efforts were made more discrete.

We learned to communicate with hand signals, patterns created in art or food, symbols placed in potted plants, musical notes, and drum beats. We could tell we were with compatriots in unobtrusive, but clear ways.

My mother believed that every person deserved to leave the prisons of illiteracy and ignorance. She had escaped a terrible fate by learning how to read. She could understand the papers that accompanied her as she was transported from farm to city. She played dumb and mute, when necessary, to hide the intelligence and comprehension in her eyes. This saved her from becoming one of the hundreds of ordinary servants who arrived in town by the train car load. My maternal homeland was famous for its meek citizens. If one needed good cooks, maids, and seamstresses, one simply placed an order and a dozen would be sent for one's consideration. Those who were rejected were simply returned to the pool of available bodies. The candidates were not allowed to object, indicate a preference, or express dismay if they were overlooked. They had no more rights than animals kept at a shelter, and only marginally more value.

My mother read the travel papers and bribed an official into assigning her to a school administrator who had four motherless children. It was a plum position. She became indispensable to the official and well-known among his acquaintances. Her responsibilities increased until she earned the rare right to receive a basic education.

The man felt it was in his own best interests, and a worthwhile investment, if his top servant could assist him in running his household. She ordered supplies, paid accounts, and helped the children with their school work.

He had no idea that she was absorbing their lessons and growing her own ambitions.

Eventually, she found a kindred spirit in the compound. My father was a professor of chemistry. She often provided him with meals if his meetings ran past the closing of the dining hall. He was a revered friend of her boss, so he was at the main house almost every day.

Their casual friendship grew into affection and blossomed into love. As a man of high position, he could choose among the women of more noble pedigree. There were many such fawning beauties mincing about. His education level had spoiled him for such banal company. He wanted to discuss complicated ideas, make observations on human nature, respond to current events, and be tickled by witticisms. He was bored by superfluous conversational gambits. He wanted fleshy, passionate discussions.

Mom responded to his brilliance with a fiery mind of her own. Their mealtime banter would frequently end with both of their faces beaming.

Their marriage was easily sanctioned by the administrator. He had watched their bond develop over time. He knew she was not just a social climber. He was fond of them both and knew that he would lose a good friend if he stood against them.

I was born into this academic stronghold and pampered by all its educated constituents. I could read, count, argue, and compose music by my fourth birthday. Although I was not a son, no one restricted my movements. I was so determined, I doubt they could have done so.

My mother arranged to have all the females in our compound meet during the drowsy siesta hours. We arrived at the main courtyard in groups of two to four heavily draped bodies.

Under the yards of fabric, we carried fresh fruit, bottles of sweet cool tea, and small gifts for the prizewinner.

If the mid-day meal had been prepared with extra sleep-inducing ingredients, none of the menfolk were any wiser. A few women who were unsympathetic to our cause were having a nice nap as well. The planners had tried to anticipate every detail.

At the appointed time, a hush fell upon the whispering crowd. My mother strode to the center of the group, near a cheerfully gurgling fountain. She removed her head covering and smiled at everyone. We followed her example. We wanted to see.

We communicated without words. It was not prudent to be overheard at this crucial juncture.

There was a flurry toward the back of the courtyard. A young woman of proud bearing was being pulled forward. Sophia had been selected!

Her hair had just begun to grow back. Its soft curls framed her intelligent gaze. She threw her head back and raised her arms. We all knew that she had earned this honor by being clever and determined. She represented the fulfillment of daring visions.

A pure white feather was held before Sophia's face. An inkwell was opened and the quill end was dipped into it. One drop of the purple liquid was used to write her name on the inside of the fountain.

The significance was not lost on anyone there. She could read anything that spoke of her. She had the ability to sign legal papers. Sophia had leashed the power of written language.

One by one, we greeted her, presented our gifts, and felt energized by her presence. This was a day that every ally would recall with exhilaration.

46

As the last person hugged Sophia and moved back to the circle, we threw our arms toward the skies and gave a silent cry. The secrets nestled within symbols were in our reach.

Sophia's name was washed away by the fountain's spray, but its power was indelible.

TICK TOCK

She opened her email during a hurried lunch, grabbed furtively at her desk. What have we here? A missive from our writing sponsor?

"Show, don't tell."

Lost in thought, she wondered how she would ever describe the mindless minutiae of a day in which ticking measured the hours of her unambitious life.

A phone rang on her desk and she scrambled to find it underneath packets of soy sauce, crumpled napkins from the corner bakery, and a sticky pack of sales meeting minutes.

"Hello, Store from Hell, where unspeakable objects are sold at ridiculously inflated prices! How may I misdirect your call?"

"I found one of your sales flyers on the bottom of my bird's cage. All I could read was the telephone number. I was curious because my budgie seemed to like speckling the monochromatic graphics. I have nothing better to do until my meds kick in."

"Yeah, well your pet has good instincts. There's nothing else on that brochure worth noting. What kind of meds are you on?"

"Umm, not sure. A bottle of a questionable nature was in my neighbor's trash bag. It fell out while I was digging up, uh, I meant, cleaning the alley. I ought to feel the results in about ten minutes. I polished off the pills with my morning beer."

I sighed heavily and hung up the phone. It was good to have some distractions. That broke up the afternoon for me. Only 14,323 more clicks until my next break.

SILENT THUNDER

Chicago summers can be muggy, with humid air clinging to the skin like a damp fleece blanket. That July, I wore my winter parka with the hood loosely covering my face. It was easier to sweat my brains out than to have them bashed from my skull.

There were bullies at my school who made me feel like the slowest gazelle in the herd. I knew that they would take me down if they found me alone and vulnerable.

So, I used the coat to become anonymous. It made me look bat-shit crazy. Maybe that saved my life?

**

That kid over there, he must be a – how you say it? – oh yeah, a psycho. It gotta be 100 degrees outside. The rest of us, we be wearin' Dago T's and sunglasses. He be walkin' around with a goddamn furry hood! Used to be fun to kick his ass. Now, we let him alone. No fun messin' with a head case.

One time, when we first seen him, we tol' him his shirt look funny. He got scared and we chased that mofo two blocks. Good times. My boys remember dat night. They say, "Hey,

Lobo, dat be one fast run!"

Now dude just keep his head down. We let him go.

**

It was 8th grade. Every gym class, I had to stay out of the way of a tall, thin girl who hated my guts. She would call me names, make the other kids mock me, and push me around. The teacher never saw her do it. I was afraid to complain. I thought she would get worse. Right before class, my stomach would start to hurt and I could feel my palms sweating. I wished I could pretend to be sick. Didn't have to do much playacting! I really did want to throw up.

One day, she came up behind me and whispered in my ear, "I ain't gonna be mean to you no more."

I was thunderstruck. I tried not to show how startled I was – or how relieved. I just kept walking, thanking all the saints that I was spared.

She never did anything cruel to me again. I never got an explanation. She ignored me after that. I had no idea why she began or why she stopped.

**

That little slanty-eyed kid was too easy to freak out. I knew I scared her, so I kept on. I liked that she would look afraid when I came in the room. I felt so cool!

At home, my ma's boyfriend waits until she goes to work or the Food Barn. If I'm still sleeping and I hear the car start up,

I run to the bathroom and shut myself in. My bedroom's got no way to keep the door closed. My brother and sister are so small, my ma says she don't want to have them get stuck in there one day. They don't like to be in the bathroom by theyselves, so we can keep a lock on that door.

If Lobo is the only one home with me, I know I got trouble.

When he started this stuff, I tried to stay awake all night. The little ones sleep so hard, they don't hear nothin'. Sometimes, I get so tired, I can't make my eyes stay open. By the time I get to school, I just want to punch something.

That little girl has a nice momma and a poppa who goes home every day. I see them pick her up from school sometimes. I hate to see her smile at them. Two brothers and a sister run in the playground with her.

When I get to gym class in the morning, her skinny eyes make me want to throw the dodge ball extra hard. Those eyes are almost black. Just like Lobo's.

**

When I was young, I had no words to express fury, agony, dismay, or terror. I knew how I felt, but did not know how to get rid of those icky emotions. I just wanted to feel better.

I was a bully because someone was using me as a scratching post.

I was a victim because I felt too weak to defend myself.

I could not make any of it stop or make healing start.

When I heard the sounds of things thudding against a wall, or a person crying hard, or a stifled scream, my soul would want to jump out of my body. I covered my ears, tried not to imagine the smack of skin against wood. I could not sob or yell. If I did, I knew I would be the next one hurting.

Years later, I met a quiet person with kind eyes. He told me that feelings are okay – good or scary. He said that I could talk about what happened. He said I was safe in that special room because everyone in there believed what I said. He held my hand and spoke softly. He never, ever hit me or used cruel words that stuck in my head and came back to me on dark, lonely nights. He brought light to a shadowy place and opened my windows. He threw the closet door off its hinges and let me peek inside. The monsters don't live there no more.

**

In the warm month of July, I take my kids for walks by the lake. We like to see the waves wipe out sand castles that we build with plastic cups and shovels. I make them wear sun hats and use a beach umbrella, but we never cover up more than necessary.

I remember that one Chicago summer when terror felt like a constant companion. It would wake me in the morning, and walk beside me as I went around my neighborhood. I finally told my mother what was happening. She cried with me. Then, we called someone and got some help.

Lobo and his boys never bothered me again. I heard later that he got shot one night. It happened in his apartment building.

Nobody was home, except his girlfriend's daughter.
Neighbors said that there was no warning. No sound.
Nothing until two loud bangs woke them up. Police found
the girl sitting in the corner of her closet. She had aimed for
Lobo's eyes, and blew the light out of them.

When I heard the news, I walked to the Catholic Church and
bought some candles. We don't attend the masses there, but
the priest lets me come and sit if I stay quiet.

It was the only place where I would take off my coat.

WASTE OF SPACE

I kept digging. The catcalls of my friends rang harshly in my ears. I started wearing ear plugs to drown them out.

The weeds lost their battle. I attacked them with dogged, steady hacks using a sharp hoe. I vowed to destroy every stinking dandelion and every stubborn blade of crabgrass. I would win!

Once they saw I could not be dissuaded, my buddies went off in search of more thrilling pursuits. It was no fun to stand in the hot sun and watch me sweat.

After my father and uncle were killed by that semi truck, the yard had gone to seed. My mother plodded through the house and had a vacant gaze. She had worn my dad's faded football jersey for the entire winter. I couldn't bear to see her slack jaw and teary face any more. I needed to see the light come back into those green eyes.

My uncle had lived in our garage apartment all my life. He had barely spoken more than five sentences a day, if you didn't count requests for the salt and extra gravy when we ate.

He communicated through the garden he had tended so
lovingly.

"There is a language of flowers," he told me. "If you look
them up in your fancy books, you'll see what each one means.
Your granny taught the secrets to me."

We had dozens of prize rose bushes and vegetables that fed
the neighborhood. Our sunflowers faced the skies and
mimicked the way Uncle Cy stretched his back and held his
chin up. He persuaded rare and wonderful herbs to thrive.
My mother's cooking was famous for its unusual flavors. She
always said the taste of our garden made her dishes
distinctive.

Mom had barely gone into the kitchen after the double
funeral.

I was sick to death of eating scrambled eggs, toaster waffles,
and bagels for breakfast. They were all I could manage before
running to school. My brothers and I had a lot of chores now
that the men were gone.

Maybe if I brought our plants back to life, my mother would
get the spark back in her eyes? If we started savoring our
meals again, maybe my world wouldn't feel so bland?

I jabbed strong tools into the dirt. Uncle Cy had been
meticulous about his garden shed implements. They were
extensions of his sunbaked arms. I had never seen a spot of

mud or a rusty metal surface in his domain. He was a tough act to follow.

The harder I worked, the lighter my mood became. After school, I could squeeze in an hour or two of weed duty. My younger siblings were too little to use a shovel or rake properly, but they could haul stuff to the compost pile for me. All five of us began clearing the property of green invaders.

Tiny shoots had begun poking their heads through the winter-weary soil. I ran to tell the household when the first daffodils came up. Lilies of the Valley filled the side of the house with their sweet fragrance. This was the scent of Spring!

My mother never acknowledged what we were doing, but she began sitting on the back porch swing. She watched us soundlessly as we labored. After a while, she would wander to the yard on her own, when she didn't think I was around, and sniff the early blooms. If she wiped away tears with muddy hands, I pretended not to notice the dark streaks.

As the first herbs came in, I snipped a few for drying and hung them from the spot my dad had built for them in our kitchen. The first time Mom walked into the room and the smell of rosemary and lemon verbena filled the air, she hesitated. She threw her head back and took in great gulps. She seemed to be drawing breath like a fish that had been released from a hook.

My hopes soared. Was she coming back?

That night, we came home from school and saw warm bread on the dining table. There wasn't a dry eye among the lot of us. We fell upon that platter as though we had never been fed. We cracked up between bites. We howled with the joy that bubbled up out of our full bellies.

My mom stood quietly in the doorway. A grin played across her lips. Her face had not formed a smile in so long, her cheeks did not know whether to poof out or make a dimple.

My littlest brother jumped out of his seat and ran to her. He flung himself around her waist and then pulled her over to the table.

The rest of us leapt to our feet and began dancing around her. She finally let out a huge whooping sound. We all were surprised by the rusty bray. She was as startled as we were!

We declared that this was the most delicious bread ever created by human hands. She p'shawed and waved away our compliments, but we insisted. We vied with each other for the most ridiculous descriptions. We roared with relish at our own wit.

It felt so good to be happy!

Mom collapsed in a chair. She gasped when she noticed that it was Dad's place at the head of the table. We had kept that spot vacant, as though Elijah would be arriving at the Seder feast sometime soon.

She saw our worried faces and held out her arms.

"No more wasted spaces, my children! We are to use all the seats, the whole fertile garden, and every joke we can think up from now to forever. Are you with me?"

Five youthful voices cried out in unison, "No more wasted space!"

We pulled, carried, hugged our mother until she followed us out to the backyard. We showed off the neat rows and tender buds. We welcomed every blooming thing.

Jo-Jo Tabayoyong Murphy

UNWAVERING COMPASS

If a goose intuits where to go and who it is, why can I not trust my own yearnings, certain I know where I belong?

COMMENCEMENT

Today, I choose to open my eyes
even though they sting,
have crusty lids,
and feel much better
when they are shut lightly.
My gaze will be appreciative.

Today, I will not take stock
of every stumble,
every blunder,
every fumble,
I may have made,
especially if I know
I did not mean to cause
anyone else's suffering,
or my own.

Today, I will breathe in
sweet oxygen.
I will catch those instances
when I am stilled
by wonder,
bliss,
excitement,
and awe.

Today, I will loosen my limbs.
I will luxuriate
in my ability to grasp at straws and
stroke my loved one's hand.
I will caress
the silky softness
of a puppy's ear.

Today, I will notice
when a stranger
lifts my spirits
with a lopsided grin,
a door is held open,
waiting
as I juggle bulky packages
and heavy burdens,
or a gallant opening
is granted
as I join the flow of heavy traffic.

Today, I will relish
a burst of spicy goodness
in the bowl of soup
that my beloved stirred into being.
I will allow the crisp layers
of a fragrant pastry treat
to linger on my tongue.

Today, I will notice
that song heard faintly
in the background
as I walk on the bustling
streets of my village.
I will recall that it played
on the day I first
sat firmly in a sailboat
slicing through foamy waves.

Today, I will bask
in the warm circle of light
provided by my desk lamp,
illuminating the stacks
of images,
quotations,
textured papers,
and array of fine-tipped markers
that will transform a thought
into a tangible, three-dimensional
missive
meant to reach
a friend who needs to know
that I am remembering
why we love each other.

Today is mine,
and yours,
and ours,
and ready
to take shape.
Today, I am awake,
alive,
astonished,
aware.

Today, I am present.

LIGHTNING

The staccato tap of raindrops hitting my window woke me
up. The grumbling of thunder soon filled the room. One after
another, deafening bursts of lightning blasted. The storm was
filling the sky, my room, and my ears. It sounded like a plane
had crashed in our backyard. The loudest boom broke from
the sky while I lay in bed snuggling under my quilt, which
protected me from the chaos happening outside. Still another
loud crack came out of the sky, mightier than the rest, into
my once quiet room. The faint sound of sirens entered the
scene, growing in intensity, as they sped to their destination.
The possibilities were frightening. More ambulances
followed, shattering the calm silence of the morning.

The last time I saw my parents, they were running outside to
close the doors of our barn. A latch had come undone and
they were afraid the animals might dash out in fear or some
other type of wild thing would find refuge inside the warm
space.

I cowered in my bright pink bedroom. Nothing could happen
to me if my panda bear Lolly, rag doll Andy, and fluffy down
comforter surrounded me. I sang quietly to myself. "Jesus
loves the little children, all the children of the world." The
night light glowed and made pretty patterns on the ceiling.

BANG!

The lights and sounds of my familiar room dissipated in an instant. "Mummmmmy! Dadddddddeeeeee!"

I couldn't see whether they were nearby. When I got startled, my bear and doll fell off the bed. I would have to take my head out of the cloth cave to see where they went. That was *not* going to happen.

A low humming began. It was faint, but I thought it was coming from the hallway outside my room. I had left the door open so I could see the front of the house, but nothing was visible through the flannel.

"Old McDonald had a farm, E-I-E-I-O."

The humming got louder as I sang. It seemed to echo my wavering soprano. Why were my folks not here to save me?

Would *I* have to rescue *them*?

I was not allowed to touch the telephone. Last month, I had played with Mummy's cell phone and a lady talked with funny words. Daddy's mouth looked like he had eaten sour persimmons when our mail came the next week. Lolly, Andy, and I spent a while in the corner of the kitchen while my folks talked about security codes and high-up hiding places.

The humming became scratchy and I stopped breathing. I could not scream because I did not want this monstrous thing to find me. Was anyone ever going to come back? Who would cook my sunny-side-up and toast in the morning? How would I go to the bathroom by myself in the pitch black house?

A loud whistle shocked me out of my silence. It would not stop. This was too much. I started sniffling, then the tears began sneaking through my eyelashes. I could not sing. I could not move. I should not cry. I was five years old! No one in my kindergarten class would believe that I had spent the night alone in my house.

Wait a minute! Lolly and Andy must be scared to pieces. I had to find them and bring them into my safe bed. I poked one arm out of the covers and felt for their softness. Ah, Lolly had not gone far. Andy must be on the other side. My fingers caught his yarn hair and yanked him up. Okay, I could face anything now.

It became easier to rest quietly and settle down. I realized that the whistle was our teapot. Mommy must have put the kettle on before she ran outside. A hot cup of cocoa would be really good.

I heard my Daddy's soft rumbly voice. He could always make Mummy laugh, even when she looked tired. The kitchen door squeaked open. Daddy said he would never fix it because he wanted to know if I was sneaking out to pick flowers. Silly Billy.

"Alice, are you awake?"

"I am right here, Mummy! I can't see anything."

The wide, bright beam of our lantern gave the hallway spooky shadows, but I was no longer afraid. I knew Daddy would soon scoop me up and take me into the kitchen. I heard the metallic clink of a teaspoon against the Hershey's Cocoa tin. We would be sharing treats in a minute.

Daddy's curly red hair looked like it was in flames as the candlelight flickered. It was the most beautiful sight I had ever seen!

"Hey, little miss, how about some of your favorite marshmallows in a big blue mug of chocolate?"

"Yay!"

I rode on my dad's shoulders while carrying Lolly and Andy. Mummy smiled when she saw us. We drank cocoa, ate butter cookies, and talked about the big storm for a little while. I started to yawn. I wanted to stay up until the birds sang, but I knew I could not do it.

As they were tucking me in, the lights suddenly came back on. We all gasped. My eyes hurt from the shiny bulbs. I asked my daddy to turn off the night light.

"Aren't you worried about sleeping in the dark?"

"Not anymore! I spent the whole storm by myself and nothing happened. I do not want that baby light in my room. It keeps Lolly and Andy awake."

My parents smiled at each other and held hands as they left the room. I sighed and burrowed under my soft quilt. As I fell asleep, I heard the rain begin its tapping against my window. This time, it sounded like an old clock instead of the angry clucking of a hen.

FULL OCTAVE

"Must not tug too hard or sparkle."

"You're right. No glimmering."

"This adept is elusive. She does not want anyone to know that she has abilities. We must be very clever if we are to capture her attention and entice her to follow us."

"I leave that to you, Aura. This is your area of expertise."

"Ah, many thanks, Corona. You are too kind and far too humble."

"Prism talents are rare. They are aware of spectrum categories and are able to spot an adept from the slightest gesture, creation or conversation. We need them more than we do the pure spectra types. We have already recruited 21 harmonic members. If we were to bring even one strong Prism into our group, we would win this challenge, Aura. The chase has intensified."

"A full octave team is wondrous to behold, is it not? I have only seen one of them. They created the solar system in quadrant 622. I watched them work together during my training. We could see the glow of their planets from a distance of ten light years."

"My mentor helped put that crew into place. She said that they had to go through 10,000 prospects to find the Prism. It was discovered by chance as they walked past a school yard. The Prism was playing tag with a dozen kids."

"Perhaps we will be that fortunate on this beautiful planet?"

"Let us set our intentions high, Aura!"

Meanwhile, at the Art Museum, Calista worked on the inventory of new pieces that had been delivered last week. She marveled at the intricate wood work on the Balinese door. It would suit their Pacific Island display very well. Her assistant, Troy, wheeled in a large crate that had come from France. The two of them worked quickly to remove the packing material. Once the canvas was uncovered, they gasped at the colors and brush strokes of a little-known Monet. What a coup it had been to win this at auction!

The upcoming show would highlight this masterpiece. They were already getting requests from all over the world for tickets to the exclusive opening night. The income from that event would be able to cover their expenses for the next three years. Everyone in the museum was making sure that every detail was perfectly executed.

Calista hummed the melody from Beethoven's Violin Concerto. She had attended a niece's rehearsal during her lunch hour. The performance was going to be astonishingly good.

She and Troy carefully directed the movers as the art work was placed in its new setting. Once it was mounted behind its security panels, they went on to the next crate. It would be a long night.

Aura and Corona felt a tug as they drove by the museum. They looked at each other with jubilation. Somewhere in that building, they might find the Prism they had sought!

Each Spectra gleams with a pure color that only a Prism can see clearly. There is also a vibrational note that a Prism with auditory ability is able to hear. Most Prisms have the talent to view colors. Very few had the discerning ear that helped hone in on the Spectra's special skill.

Search teams were equipped with ocular and aural devices that mimicked a Prism's abilities, but they were not as reliable or as sensitive as a real Prism. For broad searches, the devices were good at weaning out weaker talents.

The leader of a search team wore a piece of jewelry that showed which spectrum members had been recruited already. This helped everyone remember what they needed to find. To an unknowing observer, the bracelet, necklace or collar looked like an ordinary item, such as a charm bracelet or elaborate watchband. To other search teams, they were taunting displays of how far ahead or behind they were in their own gathering.

Aura's bracelet had all the gemstones but two: orange and violet. The large pyramid piece was also missing. There was a musical quality to her movements because the dangling pieces sounded harmonic tones as they struck each other.

Last month, they had come upon a team leader who had
chosen the shape of a Golden Retriever on this planet. Its
collar held five of the eight gem stones and a completed
pyramid piece. It had been frustrating to know that the rival
group had already gotten its Prism. That would make it much
easier to find the remaining Spectra. The knowledge that their
team could fill its dance card and leave the planet soon was a
strong incentive for Aura's team members to step up the
pace.

Once a Spectrum Card was complete, the array of prospects
was taught how to work in harmony. A short introduction
was given on their home planet. Then, the whole team was
brought to our headquarters so that their natural talents could
be honed, then broadened to complement the others in their
octet.

There was another strong pull from the north side of the
street. Aura gave a slight tilt to her head so that Corona
would know where to follow. The two of them casually
moved toward the building's courtyard. In its center, a young
boy with a mop of unruly black hair sat and played with a pile
of smooth stones. The design he created was intricate. They
could not believe that it was able to hold together without
adhesives or mortar. As soon as he built it to a height of
about two feet, he knocked it over and crowed with
exuberance.

The adepts sighed at the waste of the design, then were
startled as he began stacking and moving the stones together
to form another magnificent structure. This truly must be the
Spectra that had called out to them.

The two of them began humming, first in unison, then in thirds, then in complex harmonies, and finally back in unison. The kid did not acknowledge them, but he joined their musical line by adding his own note to the chords. Aura led the melody into meandering rhythms, soaring high, then resonating low. He kept up and even added a thrilling counterpoint.

As they harmonized, he kept building his structure. It seemed to mimic the construction of the wordless song. Aura and Corona could hardly breathe, but they continued humming their elaborate composition.

Eventually, they were within a few feet of the little one. The three of them held one last, sweet note and faded into a companionable silence.

He turned to look at them. "That was fun! I have never tried that before."

Aura asked, "Did you like that? Shall we try another song?"

"I'm not supposed to talk to strangers. Matron will get upset with me and I won't get dessert tonight."

Corona quickly replied. "May we speak to Matron? We don't want to get you into trouble."

He raised his head and gave a sharp whistle. A woman with bouncing gray curls and a big smile poked her head out of a window. "What's up, young Apollo?"

"These two ladies want to talk to you, Matron."

"I will be right there. Give me a minute to turn off the stove."

Aura and Corona put on their warmest smiles and consciously emanated positive energy.

"Hello, I am Francesca, Director of this orphanage. How may I help you?"

"We are representatives of a school of arts and sciences in South America. It is like your Juilliard school. We happened to be passing the playground. As we hummed a song, Apollo here joined us and made our simple melody into an exquisite composition."

Apollo had stopped paying attention to us when Francesca arrived. His rock tower had become even more elaborate and he gave it his full concentration.

Francesca looked at him with great fondness. "Our boy inherited some amazing artistic genes from several generations of musicians. Without lessons or much guidance, he is able to play several instruments, memorize pieces, and create his own work. We are very proud of him."

"Has he no family then?"

"Unfortunately, he is a refugee and the only surviving member of his extended family. They lived on a compound that was shattered in a battle to take over their village."

The two adepts gasped. This could not have been more fortuitous! He had been spared and that blood line could continue.

Francesca blushed, "Where are my manners? Would you like to come inside for some tea? Apollo, are you hungry? Will you please show these guests where they may wash their hands?"

Dusting himself off, the boy grinned and took them through intricately carved double doors.

The four of them shared delicious cinnamon rolls, tea, and conversation for an hour. It was as though they were old friends who were reuniting after years apart.

In the end, Apollo was brought onto Team 143. Arrangements were made for his instruction, financial needs, and comfort. Calista and Troy became his most trusted mates on this gleaming planet. The pull Aura and Corona had felt from this block had come from them as well. They won the orange and purple spaces.

Aura and Corona proudly wore their newly completed sets and gave the three new members their own symbols. Apollo opted to have an array of seven gleaming precious stones, suitable for stacking into towers, and a shining pyramid in which they could be stowed.

The spectra from quadrant 143 is developing a new grouping of stars. If you look at the eastern horizon just before dawn, you can see them sparkling.

LOVE AND LIGHT

We had met a few moments before, but I already sensed something special about this person. I shifted position so that I could see her face to face. She told me how much she enjoyed sculpting. As she spoke, I saw colors swirling from her arms. They were little particles in shades of indigo. What was going on? She told me how she looked at a face and got inspired. I was listening to her speak, but the whirling particles were a little distracting. She kept carving the marble as we talked. When she polished a detail, the indigo glimmered and shone.

I walked away from our conversation feeling as though I'd just witnessed a little magic trick.

My friend and I were meeting for lunch. I walked over to the outdoor café and saw her writing in a journal. When our eyes met, I suddenly noticed that there were colorful particles streaming from her writing hand. They were green and very bright. She smiled and the colors seemed to intensify. I rushed over to her table and gave her a hug. I asked what she was writing about. While she described the topic, the colors seemed to emanate in waves from her right hand.

What was making these bursts of light visible?

When she put down the pen, the colors faded and then disappeared. She gave a soft sigh and asked what was new.

I described a performance I'd had the night before. I played cello for a fundraiser. I swept my hands in big arcs to describe the shape of the Tiffany window at the Chicago Cultural Center. That's when I noticed that orange particles were flowing from my fingers. Oh my goodness! I could do this magic trick, too! I told the story of one point in the concert when the entire hall was silent except for my solo. It was an awesome feeling to know that the lone sound in that huge room was coming from my instrument. As I spoke, the orange bits seemed to glow and move in a rhythmic way. I got more enthusiastic when I saw my friend's face mirror my joy. The light particles seemed to move from my fingers to her eyes.

This was incredible.

Had I gotten a super power? Had my eyes taken on a new ability with this pair of glasses that I'd just picked up yesterday? I put them on when I got out of bed. I'd done my daily meditations already, so I was ready to face the morning. I hadn't noticed anything different until now. Of course, I hadn't really spoken to anyone before I met the sculptor.

I remembered then that I'd contemplated the idea that each person has a unique gift to share with the world. Could that have opened my eyes?

I decided to test this. I asked our waitress whether I could speak to the one who had created this meal. I told her that I enjoyed my dessert so much that I wanted to compliment the pastry chef. She brought the young woman over to our table. She blushed when I told her that the cake was light, fluffy, delicious, and beautifully made. I asked her where she'd learned such skills. She told me quietly that she'd taken night classes at a local cooking school and practiced making miniature cakes using her kids' Playdoh. She had always loved to make small versions of food. The tiny creations amused her family and they'd urged her to make a living doing what she adored. I watched her hands and yellow sparkles came from the palms.

This new ability of mine was fantastic!

I decided to talk to my friend about all this. She would understand. She and I shared an interest in mystical ideas. We thought about what the colors could mean. Could they be linked to chakras? The seven chakras correspond to the seven colors of the rainbow. Each chakra has its own part of the body. The colors I'd seen were indigo, the eye chakra; green, the heart chakra; yellow, the stomach chakra; and orange, the gut chakra. The sculptor visualized her subjects. My friend the writer used words that came from her emotions. The chef made fanciful pastries that satisfied the cravings of her patrons. I made music using my creative center.

I was thrilled. Now I could understand what I was seeing. I knew there was a reason for all this happening. Perhaps I was given the knack of seeing a person's true talents? That would be helpful for someone who wondered whether they should make a career change, follow their longings or invest the time and effort to pursue more studies in a field.

It would also be good for encouraging someone who felt that they had no gifts – nothing to contribute to a world thirsting for the particular flavor of water that they alone could provide.

GESUNDHEIT!

They tell me I'm sick.

I say my body is regrouping. I consider this a fallow season for me and my cells.

Health is a relative condition. I exist on a gradient. I am stronger some Tuesdays. I am lethargic some Mondays. Every Wednesday I feel better. That's always been my favorite day of the week!

I have a team of healthcare providers. I think they should wear the colors of Manchester United. At least I could recognize them in the hospital cafeteria and buy them a pudding.

We have regular assessments to discuss whether my treatments are effective. I insist that we meet after 11 a.m. If I have to wake up before then, of course I am going to feel wiped out! No respectable person should have to be presentable early in the morning. I am more cheerful mid-day. I am at my peak around 2 a.m., if I'm honest.

We would never have a conflict scheduling a conference room at that hour!

I had a sweetheart until my diagnosis. The prospect of watching me fade away wasn't appealing, I suppose. I am keeping my options open. Now that I am moving in the same

81

circles as celebrated doctors, specialists in their fields, my prospects are much better!

With all the examinations, people have seen my bits and bobs. They don't judge scars. Some of them caused a few, which they point out as their best work.

I used to wonder whether I would be famous. Would I ever be on a magazine cover? Would I walk the Red Carpet and pose for photographs? I can proudly say I have been in countless articles, training films, and textbooks. My pictures are shown to medical students around the globe. My notoriety has far exceeded anything I could have anticipated.

There was a time when I wanted to give up. I had had enough of the experimental drugs and their freaky side effects. All of the personnel in our local emergency room knew my name. One quarantine lasted eight weeks. Netflix ran out of new material. Thank goodness for random YouTube videos, eBooks, and social media. The prognosis was bleak and so was my outlook.

I never told kith or kin that I had decided to stop fighting. I kept going to the assessments, smiling on cue, trying whatever snake oil or meditation they prescribed. I knew they were useless, but the studies were funded by grants and I wanted the scientists to have jobs a while longer.

Surrender freed my bandaged, weary spirit.

Every time I closed my eyes, I wondered whether I would see that fabled tunnel of light. I was ready to discover what was beyond the rainbow bridge.

Here's the funny part. As soon as I relinquished control, my whole being felt at ease. I accepted the ministrations of my caregivers with more grace. I noticed the special features that were added to my bedroom by my family: grab bars, a rolling table near my recliner, extra channels on cable, fresh flowers every Wednesday. I told you that was the greatest day of the week!

I started writing down the highlights of my narrowed world in a blog. It gave me something to do, especially during quiet hours when my iPad was the only light in the house. It gave me a place to speak for others who might be walking the same lonely path.

In the beginning, no one read my posts. I didn't talk about my illness with anyone close to me. I liked the anonymity of writing as Frail Frankie. I thought of myself as a real-life Frankenstein's monster because I had more artificial parts than most human beings.

Slowly, my number of followers grew. My condition is so rare, anyone who researches it eventually finds my stuff online. I had some readers who sent me witty notes. A few shared my ailment. Others had family members who had succumbed. There were researchers who were trying to figure out how to squelch this dastardly disease. We had common demons.

I think the tone of my posts must have changed when I decided to give in. Paulie in Peril began sending irreverent diatribes that made me hoot until my stomach cramped. Manic Medic suggested wackadoo cures every Friday, insisting that they would make my weekends more filthy and entertaining. Sister Not-a-Nun invited me to join her tribe of iconoclasts. "We meet at dawn, holding hands as we leap into frothy waves. Clothing optional."

I never missed a day. I answered every message, but never revealed my real name or uploaded a selfie. My identity became a popular mystery. Speculation was a regular topic on medical websites. I would chat about the elusive blogger with my clinic pals. I found the whole thing enormously entertaining!

One day, I got a private message from a reader that shook me up.

"Hey, FF, can I share a secret? I think my kid has thrown in the towel. I can't prove it, but the suspicion won't go away. There is no more spark of hope. Do you have any suggestions? Your fan, Perplexed Purple"

I had to think about my response for a while. I certainly had no lifeline to offer! Could I admit that I had also decided to stop the suffering?

"Howdy, PP! Have you thought about changing up your initials? Just sayin'. I'm sorry your kid has reached this low point. Have you thought about releasing control yourself? This bugaboo is insidious. I know! I am on intimate terms with it.

I have no magic elixir left. I smoked it yesterday. My flock of luminous toads has not produced their quota of glowing serum this week, lazy beasts.

I suggest you enjoy every moment you have with your family. None of us can tell how much time we have left. Also, look into getting a case of toads for your sparkless offspring. They come with a tube of wart remover. Peace out, FF"

I checked for replies more frequently after that. Purple and I started long threads that could go on for hours. When I got tired, I would ask for meals more often. My nurses teased me about adding diet powder to my shakes. I wondered whether I had ever met Perplexed. We had a small community, bonded by this slippery beast. I attended more social gatherings, always looking for parents who looked puzzled or kids who were nearing the end stages.

Last week, I was offered a chance to speak at a symposium in California. I was excited by the prospect. Maybe Perplexed Purple would be there?

My doctors discussed the risks. I would need at least two caregivers, special accommodations, and release forms. Did I understand what might happen?

"Look, docs, you should never tell a patient with a chronic, incurable condition that they face possible disaster from a trip to a beautiful climate. I might talk the organizers into a free trip to Disneyland! I am willing to play the Last Fondest Wish card."

My lead healer, fondly nicknamed Dr. Demento, screeched at that line. This is why she's the head of my team. She gets me!

I was in a medi-van the next day, accompanied by two burly nurses, Dr. D, my folks, and my trusty iPad.

I asked PP if the symposium was on his/her radar. That sly dog admitted to having a VIP ticket. Be still, my defibrillator-boosted heart.

My speech got a standing ovation by every attendee who wasn't in a wheelchair. Those who used canes or crutches waved them in the air. I was moved.

As I met a long line of fans, I looked for anyone wearing lavender, mauve, eggplant, Northwestern University gear, or grapes. No one confessed to being my buddy PP.

I was crushed. I had really wanted to see my elusive pen pal.

There was an obligatory banquet that afternoon. I sat at the head table with other presenters. My crew was at a table close enough to be called over for assistance. I got a request from my nurses for a meal without interruptions. Hah!

A distinguished gentleman with a perfectly pressed suit approached my parents. I glanced over, but could not watch because the person to my left was eager to chat about the latest medical developments. Blah blah blah.

A soft hand on my shoulder startled me. The guest to my right pointed to my team table. I turned and saw Mr. Natty Suit waving. I excused myself from the chatty bore.

Dr. D introduced me to Albert Aubergine. As we shook hands, it felt like the grasp of an old friend. His eyes shone with intelligence and good humor. He had already fascinated everyone at the table. Who was this guy?

They drew up chairs for the two of us. My scrappy RNs were handy like that. An interesting conversation flowed as we gave thumbnail descriptions of each other. His daughter had been stricken with unusual symptoms about four years ago. She was too weak to make the journey today. Albert had come alone, optimistic about learning new information that would give his child some relief.

My father contributed more to the discussion than I had ever heard before. It struck me that he must suffer from the loneliness and isolation of my sickness as well! My mother kept smiling and nodding her head. Her usual banter was subdued as she let her once-taciturn mate have the floor.

We talked through the whole meal. As dessert plates were being cleared, I asked for an extra serving. My nurse told the caterer that it was a challenge to keep me fed these days. I got the whole group more cake. They smiled with crumbs all over their lips.

Mr. Aubergine began his good-byes. He and my dad hugged! Can you believe it? My pops is the original prickly pear. Mum is usually the affectionate one. When he got to me, his eyes twinkled. I swear to you that flashes of light really did glow from his baby blues.

"I have an ulterior motive, Frail Frankie. I made sure to have this private pow-wow with you."

I sank into my chair. "What makes you think I am that blogger?"

He gave me a wink. "Kindred spirits know these things. Also, I recognized some of your signature phrases in your speech. No one else uses that much alliteration. You really ought to watch that."

I blushed and stammered. No one else had ever unmasked me. "Please don't tell anyone. I like staying out of the public eye."

"I will keep it low if you don't blab that I am PP."

It was my turn to give him a bone-crushing hug.

"You! I have been searching for you in this mass of humanity.

I can*not* say how happy I am to finally see you."

"I am delighted as well. You have brought light and ease to some tough valleys."

I could barely keep from sobbing. This was my confidant, confessor, and charismatic colleague. (I really must watch that alliteration habit.)

"I appreciate your lifeline as well. Do you realize that you pumped me full of optimism after I had decided to let go?"

"I surmised that after a month of correspondence. I sought help for my Esperanza and found you. I am pleased that I could return the favor.

Have you decided to keep up the fight?"

"It stopped being a battle. After I waved the white flag, I felt reassured that everything would work out in my favor. Your constant updates and entertaining messages kept me curious, active, and eager to read the next post. You have been a blessing.

I hope your daughter hangs on until a cure can be found."

"She has an indomitable will to see her father reach a doddering old age! We have our good days and bleak ones, but she has been rallying lately. I share some of your notes with her. They make her laugh and she gets stronger. I told her to keep up her energy levels so that she might be part of a clinical trial."

I had forgotten why we were there! I pulled Dr. Demento's sleeve. "I think I have your candidate for the next round!"

It has been ten years since that fateful day. I am enjoying relative good health. Dr. D is smarter than she appears. Her remarkable regimen has brought healing and succor to at least a dozen of us. Albert's daughter Espy and I have become very good friends. He does not seem to age, so she has to survive a lot longer before she can see him stumble.

My blog became a series of books, a documentary, and a powerful charitable foundation that funds research.

My dad hugs more often. My mom doesn't chatter nervously anymore. They both seem more relaxed. I taught them the benefits of surrendering.

DELAYED RESPONSE

The old book had sat on the shelf of the flea market stall for the past eight weeks. Every time I wandered over to my neighbor's booth, it caught my eye, but I did not want to make my interest obvious. Other shoppers had asked about it, but she told everyone that it was waiting for just the right person.

I called her. "Hey, how's business today? Were you able to sell that collection of leather pigs?"

"Yes, ma'am! I told you that pig people can't resist a complete set. They're strange, but they keep me afloat. I sure don't want to become known as the farm animal paradise, but I do like a regular clientele."

"Good on ya! I saw a couple of older people this morning and I told them that you had just gotten a family of piglets. They rushed over to see you as soon as they heard."

"Hey, I owe you one for that! They gave me enough cash to close a little early today. Come on over and pick out something for yourself!"

That was all the invitation I needed. "Hon, watch our register for me, please? I'm going over to Lydia's."

I pretended to look over her bracelets and earrings, working my way over to the bookshelf slowly.

"That emerald and silver bangle would look fantastic with your silk dress! Have you seen it?"

"Hmm, it *is* very unusual. You know I like things to be handmade and unique. That's a possibility."

"I just brought in a carved plant stand. Didn't you tell me you'd just gotten an orchid the other day?"

"You have an amazing memory, Lydia. My mom gave me a pretty iron holder the other day. Good idea though.

"What about this book? I like the leather cover. It would really add a nice touch to my collection."

"Funny you should ask. When I first saw it at an estate sale, I thought of you. Look at the dedication page."

I gasped when I read, "For all the times you wondered whether I remembered, Jo." I flipped to the title page and felt a little faint when I saw that it was written by my old flame. He had died five years before. We had lost touch, but mutual friends had let me know the shocking news. I never knew he had gotten anything published.

"We knew each other about thirty years ago. This is quite a surprise. Did you ever read it?"

"I'm more of a romance novel fiend. Biographies bore me. You're welcome to take it. Not only did you do me a huge favor today, I think this was meant for you to find."

I thanked Lydia and held the wrapped book tenderly. How could I maneuver my packed hours to include time to read this? I would have to do it soon. I knew there were messages in this story that were meant for me.

I walked quickly back to our booth and slipped the book into my satchel. If it made my co-worker curious, she gave no sign. We were so busy for the next few hours, I almost forgot about my purchase.

The gongs of the church clock tower signaled the end of our shop day. The two of us quickly flipped the sign to read "Closed. Find treasures another day." Honey looked tired and was probably hungry. She had covered for me during her regular break, so she had not had time for an afternoon snack.

I waved her off. "Go home to that rowdy family of yours! I'm sure dinner is already waiting on the stove."

She looked grateful as she grabbed her purse and raced out the door. I'm sure she wanted to beat the traffic.

I quickly closed out the register and straightened everything for the next morning's staff. I put the kettle on and settled down in the back room with my treasure.

How was that long-ago conversation going to end?

GREEN

The mountains presented themselves in the restaurant window in simple splendor. Trees standing near the building provided a contrast to the other four shades that touched three bumps in the earth. I shot picture after picture, trying to capture that rich crazy quilt of shapes and shadows. Nothing satisfied my eye.

When we drove away from this place, I knew I could not recreate that drama. I am not a painter. My canvas of white paper, black ink, and inadequate words would never be able to reproduce this view that held me. Disregard the glaring gas station price list. Look away from the battered truck that passed by. Keep counting the ways in which nature responded to light, foliage, angles, and sparkle. Snap photos until the sun moves across the sky and stops providing the interaction necessary to create this incredible variety of greens.

I looked away for a moment to check the battery on my phone and the scene shifted. The vivid yellow-green, green-yellow, forest green, speckled emerald, and dusky gray-green lost their luster.

The picture that would have inspired Georgia O'Keefe is

nothing more than the view outside a steak house in a small mountain town. I felt a loss.

A wondrous land had existed for three minutes. No one will ever be able to see it again.

A picture paints a thousand words, but a thousand words cannot paint a picture.

THE GLOW OF WELL-BEING

When the sun set, our home was plunged into inky darkness. We rushed as the horizon began to glow because we knew that brightness was fleeting. Noses were counted. Food was put away, keeping it from the curious eyes and hungry mouths of wandering animals. My little brothers and sisters snuggled on blankets and woven mats. My mother used a big leaf to fan us as we closed our eyes. My father put up the barrier in front of our door. He slept closest to it so that he could react to any outsiders.

I fell asleep knowing I was safe, warmed by the presence of the ones who loved me best.

We did not know we lacked any luxuries. We did what was necessary to eat, keep clean, and banish pesky creatures. My memories of that time are filled with happiness, a sense of contentment, and upbeat thoughts. Sunset brushed away sharp lines and hard edges. Everything looked fuzzy and soft in the shadows, but I looked away from them. I was a bit fearful of the night.

My parents were inseparable. They had escaped to this area with the rest of the villagers after their childhood homes were destroyed by a volcano. I took their devotion, partnership, and love for granted. I thought all couples were as entwined as they.

After giving birth to her eighth child, my mother developed a fever. My father gave her the herbs that our local midwife recommended. I shepherded my siblings so that she could rest. In the evening, I began fanning us, especially my restless momma.

Three days went by. My father decided that he could not rely on our local healers. He had heard of a modern doctor who had a small clinic at the foot of our mountain. I promised that we children would be fine while they were gone. Our neighbors were not far if we were in need.

We had a small horse cart. We borrowed blankets and tucked my sick momma behind the seat. My auntie held my shoulders as we all waved good-bye. I tried very hard not to cry. I knew that the others looked to me for my response to this distressing situation. My baby sister went with our kind relatives. There was a wet nurse there who could keep her healthy in my mother's absence.

I will never forget that early, early morning. My father sat in the front of the cart with his head looking forward. He raised a hand to wave farewell, then clicked for our horse to move. My mother could not open her eyes.

It felt as though all the light in my world went with them. I led the little ones into our hut and gave them their breakfast. No one spoke. I could barely swallow. The rest of the day stretched out before us, gloomy and discouraging.

I shook my head. My folks were relying on me. I had to lift us out of these sad depths. I decided we would do something useful.

Clapping my hands, I asked all of my trembling family members to finish their food quickly.

"We are going to tidy the house, then we will make our yard look pretty!" I pointed to the three oldest kids. "You will collect all these dishes and wash them. When you are done, please weed the garden. Collect the ripe vegetables." They nodded eagerly. The littlest ones begged to have something assigned. "You will fold the sleeping blankets. Then, you will go outside and clear out any leaves or branches that are covering the walkway. We will all feed the chickens and pigs." They jumped up from the table with smiles on their faces.

I decided that I would collect firewood. It might be wise to ask our nearest relatives if I could have some of their stash. They would be glad to help us. There was a camaraderie here that was forged by years of interdependence and good humor.

The sun rose in a bright blue sky. I heard birds chatter as I invaded their sanctuary outside the edge of our property. I sang to them that I only needed a few of the branches that had fallen.

In a few hours, our home looked lovely. My sister had picked a few flowers and put them on the table. My brother stacked all the dishes in the cupboard and collected the cloths we had used to cool my mother. I helped him scrub them clean and hang them on the wash line. They waved like brave flags. They boosted our spirits and looked like festival decorations.

One by one, our neighbors dropped by to see whether we
needed anything. They brought us sweet treats, simple meals,
and kind words. I received many hugs. I checked to see how
my newest sister was doing. She was fast asleep in my
grandfather's arms. I knew that we would survive this crisis.

As the horizon began its evening changes, I herded the
children into our hut. We did the nightly routine and that
calmed us down. My brother was able to barricade the door
with my help. All of us sank into our places, tired from a busy
day. When the sun dipped below the tree line, we were ready
for sleep. I positioned myself near the doorway.

The next afternoon, I kept us to similar tasks. I did not know
how long it would take for my parents to return.

My mother and father returned after four days. The look of
relief and pure joy made my father's entire being shine. I
think I could see his aura long before I spotted the familiar
bobbing head of our horse. My mother was seated beside
him, leaning on his shoulder. She had a soft smile on her pale
face. He held her tightly with one arm as he guided the
horse's reins with the other.

When they arrived, I shrieked to the whole village that they
were back! All of us raced down the road to meet them,
shouting words of welcome. They rode up to our home and
grinned as they saw the results of our hard work. My auntie
rocked the baby and gave her to my mother's outstretched
arms. My father picked each one of us up and spun us
around. The two of them praised us for being so resourceful
during their absence. I could not stop crying. I think all the

apprehension and sadness I had held in was finally able to escape.

That night, after the last villager had left our hut, we started to do our daily routine. My parents motioned for us to sit down. They had a surprise! From the back of the wagon, they brought out lanterns. Our mouths gaped, then we crowed with excitement.

The night would no longer dictate its limitations. We were people who had harnessed light! We could study lessons in the evening, play games indoors, and linger over meals.

This was fifteen years ago. That week is wrapped in the glow of recollection. After that, I was able to look into dark corners without fear.

POWDER AND DUST

Do you dream in color?

When I read, the words shimmer and glow like light reflecting off a floating soap bubble.

My mother taught me how to write using sidewalk chalk on our circular driveway. I spent long summer days on my hands and knees, filling the cement with the alphabet, simple stories, and drawings that illustrated my tales.

When my father arrived in the evenings, he would hold my grubby hand while we walked along the semi-circle I had adorned. Sometimes, if dinner was already made, my mother would hold my other hand. They would swing me between them as I recited. We would make up music to go with the text. Dancing could erupt spontaneously!

My grandparents adored me. They would drop by after their evening meal so that I could show them my work. Their phones are filled with videos and pictures of my creations. We eventually transferred these hours onto DVDs and hardcover books: he life of an only child as immortalized by doting family members.

Rainy days were spent indoors. I had a wall-sized blackboard in my playroom. It was barely big enough to hold my sloping sentences. I used a step stool to reach the highest bits. My lungs must have been coated by those fine powdery clouds.

Mom dressed me in plain white. That made it easier to bleach away the rainbow film that covered me. She tied a kerchief over my braids. On windy afternoons, I grabbed my swim goggles so that I could scribble without going blind. I was devoted to my task.

That is how I spent my fifth summer on the planet. Hours and weeks flew by. I only paused to have picnic lunches in the shade of our gazebo. I would talk to my rapt parents about the characters who acted out my whims. The star was usually a young girl who looked a lot like me. She was intrepid, venturing into danger without hesitation, despite legs that trembled or eyes that grew wide with anxiety. My alter ego had the confidence that I was still developing.

Outside of my family circle, I was silent and bashful. We lived on a block without children my age. Our neighbors commuted. If they waved at me, I never noticed because my focus was on the rough surface of our wide driveway.

Kindergarten was an unwelcome interruption. My teacher was sweet and kind, but she had many of us in her classroom. I was accustomed to having an adult's complete attention. The other kids seemed clumsy and ill-behaved. I longed to get back to my house so that I could write down the ideas that bumped around my brain.

My skills were not on par with my fellow students. They were still learning to form basic shapes. I was manipulating a corral of long words. They talked about cartoons. I told them my own plots. I stuck out. They blended together.

No matter. I could endure a few hours of forced socialization as long as I could return to my own pastel-hued universe.

During the parent-teacher conference, the topics discussed seemed to worry my folks. They knew I was clever and had the potential to absorb schoolwork easily. The withdrawn little girl who inhabited my classroom seemed far removed from the engaged, animated one they knew. They did not want the primary school experience to smother my creativity or halt my development.

They sought alternatives. That is how I became a pupil of Madame Belleza. She had a welcoming studio that overlooked the riverbank. Its curved windows formed an entire wall. No matter what the weather was doing, her work room was bright and luxurious. I clapped my hands with excitement as soon as I walked in.

Madame B had always lived here. Perhaps the streets and citizens formed around her elegant home because people were drawn to her vivacious energy. Her property was at the core of our downtown. Everyone knew where it was. Visitors could spot it as they approached from miles away. Boats made regular trips past and pointed it out as a landmark. She was our favorite celebrity.

My family knew hers. Generations of our stock had formed bonds over decades. She may have given me that first box of sidewalk chalk!

I went faithfully to her classes until I was in high school. She guided my fledgling talents until my abilities matched the ambitious projects I envisioned. Her suggestions were muted. She posed questions and did not dictate instructions. I was praised softly. Parents and grandparents may have lauded my talents. Madame B would nod once or twice if she saw something that improved. Once in a while, her beaming smile would break out if a piece astonished her. I flourished under her tutelage.

The most effective teachers help others uncover what is already waiting inside them. My mentor did that for me without allowing me to become arrogant or foolishly self-absorbed.

During my senior year, we sat together at an easel. I was explaining why I had selected that particular form to give life to my latest heroine. Madame Belleza paid close attention until I finished speaking. Once she was sure I was done, she nodded once in approval.

"Now, we must talk about what comes next in your life, my dear."

I was surprised. I had assumed I could continue my lessons, perhaps even coming more often once I graduated. School continued to be a required distraction from the real purpose of my waking hours.

"Madame, are you weary of my presence? Do you want me to stop attending your classes? I hope I have not offended you in any way."

She allowed me to babble a while. My conversational skills were not as well-honed as my graphic ones. I should have sketched what I wanted to say. We normally communicated in long, pregnant pauses. A small gesture could convey paragraphs. I felt as though I needed to defend my position.

When I finally broke down into quiet sobs, she held my shoulders in two gnarled hands. When had she grown older?

"You have a rare gift. I can only lead you as far as I have traveled. You need to see a greater view so that your innate talent may be served properly."

"That is not true! You are the greatest artist I have ever known!"

She raised a hand to stop me. "Yes, I may be the highest peak you have witnessed. I tell you there are mountain ranges out in the distance that you would fall to your knees to take in. You deserve to be among the clouds, not tied to the foothills."

I still remember every phrase, each nuance of that momentous afternoon's conversation. Madame B allowed me to be nervous, ask pleading questions, argue for my limitations. In the end, we chose a handful of possibilities. I left clutching brochures describing universities and art programs that might suit me.

Over the next year, I visited these places. Sometimes Madame B accompanied me and my family if she had a colleague there. We always contemplated the balance between positive aspects and shortfalls. I got over my initial reticence. I would have been content to remain with my parents, make the short drive to that riverside studio, and keep my projects to this small world.

My mentor saw bigger worlds for me. She saw an open road, while I looked inward. Her foresight saw the future when I could only imagine this afternoon.

Nowadays, I have my own sunny workspace. I take good care of my tools and spend hours each day allowing my imagination to romp freely. My husband and I paved a large expanse in the backyard for our children to use as they wish.

One likes to draw. The other loves to bounce balls and skip rope on her plot of tarmac. They can dream, too.

Madame Belleza unveiled a portrait at my graduation party. It showed a young girl kneeling on a curved pavement, head bent in concentration. Around her, a technicolor world gleams. Clouds overhead blend with the drawn images. I had never peeked at myself from that angle.

I recognized our town, but noticed that unfamiliar lands were visible on the horizon. The girl would only need to lift her head to see them.

BEAST OF BURDEN

How did Atlas stand still
as he bore the earth
and its squirming inhabitants
on his able shoulders?

Could he hear the squabbles?
Did wars jostle the delicate balance
of rumbling mountains, sloshing oceans, and bulky cities?

What did he ponder when he could not sleep?
We have the escape of naps,
long conversations over coffee,
vacations by the seashore.

This lonely giant
had only his own thoughts for company.
No companion took over his burden
so that he could lower his arms.

Lately, I have felt crushed
by my own share of real estate.
Bearing its weight
presses upon me until
my knees buckle.

I cannot see the end
of my own Herculean tasks.

I would willingly shed
these boulders,
but they would flatten
those who cling to their slippery sides.

And so, I shift the contents
of my ragtag cargo
until I find a way to continue.

I move with gentle care
so that those riding above me
will never know
who holds them up in lofty heights.

ECHOES AND NEW REFRAINS

The dinner table feels incomplete.
Your presence at its head is missing.
Someone else says grace.

We recount familiar tales.
You used to deliver the punch lines.
We smile and often chuckle.

Our barbershop quartet is
like a three-legged dog
who has learned to move with grace.

I sing the tune we made up
as we drove along a bumpy road.
I hear your harmony from a great distance.

Some days, it is as though you are in another room.
Once in a while, I catch a glimpse of thick white hair
And I almost call your name.

I see your eyes on my grandchild's chubby face.
She arrived as you were lifting off.
Did your paths cross in Heaven?

Your knickknacks were coated with fine dust.
They went to a family whose shelves are no longer bare.
They are treasured and on display.

Remember that shabby cap you loved?
You used to wear it when you gardened.
A scarecrow now sports it at a rakish angle.

The path to your favorite fishing spot
is quite overgrown.
That clever old trout swims freely.

The maple tree you planted stands tall.
We have summer picnics in its shade.
Its leaves turn red-gold around your birthday.

I whisper secrets to you in the darkness
as I draw the curtains.
Good night, sleep tight, rest in my heart.

You have been absent for 4,256 days,
three graduations, one wedding,
and a multitude of family portraits.

We hold a place for you
and speak your name with joy.
Your fragments make us whole.

A CANDLE IN THE WINDOW

On the 6th of each month, she would go to the coast and fling something into the foamy surf. I watched her from my vantage point in the lighthouse. We never spoke. I doubt she noticed anyone else. It didn't matter how dark the clouds were, how much the tide had clawed at the cliffs, or whether rain made it perilous to walk on the slick path.

Our village consisted of a few gray stone cottages, a general store/post office, the once-whitewashed church, and my striped tower. None of the inhabitants seemed to mind the bleak scenery or the lack of modern distractions. Their cheeks were ruddy from wind that seemed to flow endlessly through the place. Women wore scarves and kept their hair plaited or pinned up. The men pulled tight hats down over their brows and walked briskly, though their posture made them look like so many candy canes sailing down the street.

I was assigned to this far-off post because I was one of the newest recruits. I had no smiling wife to drag away from her family or friends. If I were going to have offspring, I would not want them to grow up without contemporaries. The school in a neighboring village accommodated the few littles that played in a small patch of green on the high street. I suspected the families who owned land could connect their branches to the same family tree. Strangers did not venture this way. Those who did were either pushed here by their trade or desperate to leave civilization.

I had been here for five months before I found out the name of the mysterious female. I happened to mention what I had seen as I picked up my mail. The postmistress/storekeeper is a cheerful, talkative, neighborly character. She is well-suited for her work because she likes to know the welfare of her customers. She did not tell others whether a family was receiving past-due notices, but she might slip an extra bit of flour or candy into a grocery bag. If mail started to pile up, she made it her business to stop by a home to deliver it in person. She was the guardian of our village.

"That would be our Dolores. You don't need to worry about her. She has her reasons. She makes that pilgrimage because she misses someone."

I had made up all sorts of dramatic tales to account for her strange antics. Was she hiding from the law? Did she like to feed the birds that cawed hungrily? Was she a bit soft in the head? This explanation made as much sense as anything I had imagined.

The next time Dolores walked slowly in front of my lighthouse, I happened to be walking out my front door. It was not really a coincidence, though I tried hard to make it seem that way. There were very few things to keep a curious young man occupied and I had already taken care of my duties for the day.

I waved a welcome and gave her a small grin. I was surprised

111

when she returned my wave. She had to shout hello because a storm was kicking up the leaves.

I walked over to her and introduced myself. "I'm Declan, keeper of the light."

She laughed and I marveled at the sweetness of the sound. "I'm Dolores. I write books."

"Do you spin tales of mayhem or craft delectable recipes?"

"Neither. I am a mathematician. My word problems in textbooks bring fear to children and dread to parents everywhere."

That started a conversation. I invited her in for a cup of tea and some biscuits that I'd just received from my gran. Who could resist homemade chocolate chip treats? Certainly no friend of mine would!

My living quarters were spare and simple, but the fire made my kitchen look quaint and welcoming that day. We ended up chatting for over an hour. I was dismayed when Dolores glanced at the windows and noticed that the sun had set.

"Oh no! I've quite overstayed my welcome. You must have important things to do to keep ships from crashing into our coast."

"Not at all. To be honest, most of the mechanics are handled by electronic equipment. Modern times, miss! I've enjoyed the company. This village turns in early."

She smiled and I saw that her front teeth crossed in an

112

endearing way. "That makes two of us. An author leads a solitary existence most of the time. And, arithmetic doesn't make citizens curious enough to ask me about my work."

"Drop by when you can get away from devising puzzles about the velocity and number of miles it takes two trains to catch up with each other."

I walked her to my gate and watched as she headed toward the center of town. Her house was at the edge, as far away from me as it could be. I had offered to walk her home, but she told me to stay warm and dry.

In time, I hoped she would tell me what she threw into the sea with such regularity.

Perhaps we could console each other?

I chose this vocation because my soulmate had lost her life crossing an ocean. Her small boat had been caught up in a sudden squall. Losing her bearings had sent her far away from safe harbor and our apartment. Since then, I had vowed to show others the way home.

UNCONTAINED

It was the silence that I would remember from that time. The scenes in my head go by like deteriorating color photos. The objects are focused and clear, but the hues are washed out and bland. As the details fade, memories seep out of my mind.

I pore over photo albums, adhesive on their pages long dried out. The images were placed carefully so as to make the most pleasing arrangements. All was for naught. If I pick up an album, pictures fall out and the meticulously designed layouts are lost forever.

Faces caught in crowd shots are candid and raw. The subjects had no chance to mask emotions. I saw myself seated at a table, alone, head resting against my open palm, looking down at an empty plate. My eyes were shaded, but body language screamed the words I could not utter.

We were not supposed to display our family secrets in public. Hell, we kept our feelings private even within our home's brick walls. We were able to glean messages from the tilt of my mother's neck, my father's gritted jaw, my grandmother's weary sigh as she washed dishes, and the slam of a bedroom door in the early morning.

There were endless hours when we sat apart. Our house had enough rooms for each occupant to pretend no one else inhabited the place. I wore thick headphones to muffle annoying or terrifying sounds. I played stacks of record albums continuously whenever I was home. My family rarely knocked on my closed, locked door. Why bother? They were ensconced in their own sanctuaries.

When our address was a compact bungalow, we lived side by side. At night, there were more blankets and pillows on floors than there were on beds. My brothers dragged quilts into the room I shared with my sister. The four of us would talk in the darkness until we dropped off. Ghost stories, secrets, tales of schoolyard bullies, and old jokes filled the room. We tried to whisper so we wouldn't get scolded, but sometimes the giggles overwhelmed us. I loved falling asleep listening to their soft, snuffling breaths.

The new house had several segments. Stairs led to bedrooms, lounging areas, basement, and garage. We could disappear for days!

Dinners used to be rowdy affairs, with the kids vying for a moment in the spotlight and adults leading the conversation. We teased each other, creating family legends that exist to this day. I could recite our favorite dinner menus with gusto! Fried chicken went well with green beans. Flank steak sizzled with onions. Fish was fried until it got crispy and gave a satisfying crunch. The dreaded boiled beef and greens warned me with its odor. I knew to sneak a few snacks on those nights! We had more than enough food and many mouths to consume everything.

At the bigger house, dinners weren't well attended. There were rehearsals, meetings, appointments, and excuses that kept us from the common table. It was not unusual to find one person munching on leftovers at 10 p.m. More than anything, we began eating in front of the televisions in our den, kitchen, and bedrooms. Tiny images on shimmering screens became our companions. We knew more about celebrities' lives than our relatives' experiences.

Water molecules are densely packed when they get cold. Warm them up and the resultant steam disperses to fill any size of container or room. We were beyond the boiling point, so we circulated away from the locus of our home.

What keeps a family close? What draws us in? How do you rein in wild horses that have developed a taste for open fields?

SEEING WITH EYES SHUT

I pay attention when I am asleep. Dreams are my workplace. My eyes are closed, but my other senses are at full alert.

Other people have told me I must be nuts. "What do you mean? How can you be productive while you're snoozing? You must be imagining things!"

They're right about that! I am most creative when my brain has no limits.

My paycheck arrives once a week, without fail. The company that hired me does not question my methods. I give them results. That's their objective.

What do I do when I am not under the Sandman's spell? I'm just like everybody else. My clothes have to be washed. I have to eat. Friends like to invite me over. I have a full, active life.

My family doesn't see me often, however. They know I have a hyperactive sleep cycle. I embarrass them. When I was a kid, I could glance at my homework after school. I wouldn't spend any time on it until I took a long nap. I would wake up and write entire essays, solve pages of math problems, and construct science projects. It freaked out my siblings. They would stay up all night studying for tests. I listened to recorded textbooks and woke up refreshed, knowledgeable,

117

and very hungry. All that brain work taxed my physical resources!

When I would walk in the house, my grandma and grandpa would make the sign of the cross and spit. Gave me a complex! I began to sneak into my room by climbing through a basement window. Yeah, my bed was tucked in a corner, away from the washer and dryer. I could jump under my blankets, pop in a set of ear plugs, and settle down quickly. My mom made a little extra for each meal. I collected the Tupperware whenever I ran out of food. I rarely sat down to eat with the rest of the family.

Before I graduated from high school, I was recruited by a big engineering firm. My counselor gave me an enthusiastic recommendation. None of my teachers knew my regimen. Well, no one knew except Ms. Truitt. She taught biology and was the Science Club sponsor. I could talk to her about anything.

One afternoon, I admitted my unusual abilities to her. Our club was going on a three-day trip to attend a conference. I told her I would need my own room and plenty of grub. She listened quietly while I told her about my vivid dream life and isolation at home. Ms. Truitt didn't judge me. She didn't gasp or look horrified. And, she never spit after genuflecting. I sure appreciated that!

We researched my wacky habits. Her friend Dr. Somnos studies sleep. I went to his lab to be examined. My neurological tests came back normal, except for my REM sleep. The brainwaves were off the charts! Apparently, I have more neurons firing when I am in deep slumber than most folks do when they're wide awake. It's a rare condition. Only a handful of people like me have been discovered.

My kind mentor invited my parents,. counselor, the principal, and Dr. Somnos to school for a conference. It was the first time anyone had ever helped me seem normal - or at least not spooky!

My mom apologized for my grandparents' behavior. Her parents had been raised to be suspicious of those who might be full of the devil, whatever that meant.

My dad awkwardly patted my shoulder, but couldn't look me in the eye. He squirmed a lot during the conference. He is an actuary. He likes predictable actions. Aberrations offend him.

My siblings please them both. They have no, um, *special* characteristics. I am the changeling.

After that eye-opening confab, I was able to ask for extra resources in my bedroom. I begged for my own mini fridge and microwave. We even installed a window/door contraption so I didn't have to shimmy through a small window to get inside. My grandparents still did their religious mumbo jumbo, but they would wait to spit until I left their vicinity. Hey, I was glad for small favors!

I moved into my own place two days after graduation. By then, I had been doing side work for months. I saved enough dough to buy a humble abode close to the city. No roomies were necessary. I was experienced at fending for myself. The house was big enough to have pals over for a party. I had insulation put in so that I could sleep undisturbed anytime I wished.

Right now, I am devising protocols that will enable humans to make long trips into the heavens. I am concentrating on making sleep viable for months at a time. Who is better suited for that conundrum, eh?

I have a good life. You might say I am making my wildest dreams come true!

ODDS ARE

As soon as I walk into a club, I sniff that aroma and my fingers twitch. There's no place else that has the heady mixture of nicotine clouds, watery drinks, cheap lavatory soap, and unbathed customers. Smells like money to me!

I tell myself I will make one orbit around the main floor. I'm listening for the electronic bells and whooping sirens that announce winners. I won't go to *those* slots. They've already paid out. I look for the old hats who have camped out at a bank of machines. They've got their ID cards pushed into a hole to tally the times they've played the games. Some of them carry a drink in one hand, grip a lighted cigarette with pursed lips, and press the buttons with their other hand. There's a weary rhythm to their movements.

They're the pathetic ones. They've got no system. They just go 'til they have to stop.

If I can snag one of their machines as they give up, I might cash in on their despair. They could be walking away right before the bonanza!

At the card tables, the croupiers manage their players with finesse. They know how to encourage the hopeful and boost drooping spirits. This is how they earn tips and keep a customer parked on a stool.

Today I cashed my paycheck and headed to the bus station. There's a Friday night excursion that heads straight for the welcoming neon columns of this resort. Marco the driver waved as I hopped onto that first step. If I grab the seat behind him, I am the first one out. He knows I prefer that position. I'll bet he doesn't know that's the sign I'll have a winning night!

Marty didn't want to go with me. Can't understand why I insist on making the trek every other weekend. Last time, Marty came out a hundred bucks ahead, went over to the waiting area, and grabbed the next bus south.

I stayed put. The progressive machine I was feeding was close to exploding. I could feel the good juju! Marty coaxed me to go home. Nuts to that. Why leave before the miracle happens? The very next pull of the handle could be the jackpot!

I spent everything I won that time. Good thing I bought a round trip bus ticket.

Marty thinks I might need a new hobby. Can you see me growing roses or polishing figurines like an old granny?

I work hard at the restaurant. When we have a busy shift, my backpack is heavy with tip money. I take a Ziplock bag over to the grocery store and exchange it for paper bills. That's my stash.

Marty is a decent roommate. We split the utilities, but buy our own food. It's a furnished two-bedroom in a safe part of town. We started taking the Friday bus together two months ago. I like the routine.

After my reconnaissance lap around the casino, I find a place to sit at the dollar machines. My system is to play until I win a couple of hundred bucks, then move on to the five-dollar area.

I start an exciting streak where the poker hands hit over and over. I am up $600! I know I ought to advance to the more pricey slots, but this is golden.

The rush makes me want to jump up and dance, but I can't break the flow. Haven't gone to the john in a while. Shouldn't have accepted those free drinks when the progressive hit!

I can't tell how long I've been playing here. Did we get a new batch of workers yet?

I peek at my score. When did I get down to three dollars?

My hip is buzzing. Has my leg gone numb? No, it's my phone. I had it on silent.

It's Marty calling.

May as well answer. I need to get more cash anyway.

"Geez oh Pete, Marty! What's up? Whaddaya mean it's time to leave? I'm doing great!

Wait, what day is it? Can't be right. You're kidding. Shit, man. Okay. Thanks for checking on me."

I squint at my phone screen. Yup. It's Sunday noon. I lost more than my paycheck and an extra grand. Two days slipped by.

A picture of Ma crying came into my head. I had pushed that memory to the back part of my brain. She kicked me out of her house a year ago. She told me I needed help that she couldn't give.

I start moving toward the bus stop. I wonder where I can find an assortment of ceramic cats.

PRAIRIE RETREAT

I am not a real cowboy,
But I can hear cattle snuffle beside me,
See a sky salted with stars,
and click my boots across a linoleum floor.
My hips sway to the rocking of a horse's canter
as the whir of a lasso spinning overhead thrums through my
arms.
I wipe the sticky dust off my face with a worn flannel sleeve.
The grasslands whisper an invitation and fill me with longing.
I may not ride across the plains,
But my soul lives there.

LISTENING TO THE UNSPOKEN

Sometimes, I think too much.

A bully punches me in the stomach. I cry because it hurts my belly, but I weep days or years later. I wonder who taught a kid that pain solved things.

I find an old dresser on a driveway, waiting for the trash collectors to swoop it up. I want to rescue it so that the memories stuffed into its drawers don't get discarded. I ponder whether IKEA furniture will ever have sentimental thoughts clinging to it like hidden cobwebs.

I hear song lyrics and hum along with the melody. A young man wrote that tune after his desires were crushed. The first redhead he had ever kissed forgot his name three months later. He immortalized her shallow emotions with a few strummed guitar chords.

I smooth a coverlet over the squeaky mattress. The proprietor of this humble bed and breakfast counted our blueberry pancakes carefully. Each guest was served three perfectly round hotcakes. After that quota was reached, the syrup dispensers were removed from the dining tables. The hostess had pursed lips and a crisp, flowered apron. She could recite the proverbs that were cross-stitched on every sampler adorning the walls. They had glowered at her since an uneasy childhood began in this ancestral home. After four generations, she and her sister had converted it into an inn to keep from foreclosure. The glares of her family portraits judged every move.

I thank her for every gesture of kindness or service.

In school, I was admonished for not paying attention. My problem was quite the opposite. I was fixated on the shabby pant legs of my classmate Roger. I knew he had grown three inches since January and had five younger brothers waiting to wear those denims. Two older siblings had rubbed a shine into the back pockets. Where did their two little sisters get their clothes?

I could sense the stories whispered by unclipped bushes at the corner house. We didn't see much of old man Parker after his missus succumbed to that harsh cough. Newspapers mouldered on his creaky porch. I wanted to ring his doorbell and ask how he was doing, but his watery eyes and shuffling gait scared me. If we met on the street, he looked over my head and sighed mightily. I'd stand very still until he passed by.

My cousin tells me I need to get braver. My voice gives out when I talk in front of people. I see a bunch of faces and my head begins hearing their tales. That girl is mooning over the freckle-faced guy beside her. She can't hear what I am saying because her pulse is pounding in her ears. She only swallows twice a minute and blinks so fast her lashes are blurs. I forget my rehearsed speech because new words are crowding into my mind.

Some days, I put these thoughts into sentences and cram them into a book. Otherwise, I would have to keep them corralled in my brain like palominos that have never been saddled. If there were too many in the holding pen, a few would leap gracefully over the fence. Those ideas might never come back, so I hold my hands over my mouth or ears when a really good phrase comes along, hoping to keep exciting words from racing away.

Grandma says I come from a long line of storytellers. She was never formally taught to write much more than her name, but she raised fifteen kids to respect education. Some of them grew up loving books and two became authors. Grandma spent her days cooking, cleaning, changing diapers, and talking to her family about what they learned in school. I think she learned to read by sitting down in the wee hours and combing through the textbooks her kids brought home. My granddad never thought females were able to pick up on any subject outside their home chores. She had to wait until every inhabitant had fallen asleep to get some quiet time.

I have always been a light sleeper. I would sneak down the stairs and peek at my determined Grandma while she held elementary primers in her lap. With no one to guide her, and a need for secrecy, she couldn't ask anyone questions or get clarity. I surprised her one night by tiptoeing over to her chair. I volunteered to help with her studies.

She repaid me with my favorite dishes and a big birthday cake. When it was time for me to go to college, her social security check paid to hold my place at the university.

Grandma showed me I could do anything tugging at me. I remember her when my determination flags. I longed to be a weaver of stories. She could hear what wasn't said and passed that ability on to me. She told me to give my characters a chance to voice their most secret thoughts.

Sometimes I think too much, but I feel exactly the right amount.

FOLLOWING A BREAD CRUMB PATH

Wrote four,
Published three.
Lost my way
Got scared.
Followed the dollar
Instead of choosing fun.
Anxiety pushed away art.

Encouraged!
Cheered,
Patted backs,
Helped wrangle others' demons.
My monsters roamed unchecked.
Boo became boo hoo.
I could slay dragons
If their scorching breath
Singed anyone who shared my round table.

My inner naysayers
Peeked out once the moon set.
Daylight made them yawn.
They were at full strength
And pounced when I was
Halfway
Between waking

And unconsciousness.
No one took up a sword
To fend them off with me.

I resolved to sew my muse's mouth
Shut
Using a precise tailor's stitch.
Would not listen to whispers about being
Brave
Unique
A Visionary.

Decided to keep a mundane
Banal
Plodding
Routine.

I worked diligently.
I smiled too brightly.
I mopped and cleaned.
Rarely spoke.
Words
Had been my minions.
Then, they became
My betrayers.

Determined to fit in
Among the quiet and unassuming,
Those not bothered by
Flashes of intuition,
Lightning bolt ideas,
And a glimpse of what could be.

While I did chores,
My imagination
Escaped!
Wild creatures crept from underneath
My tight uniform cap.

A loud door chime
Sliced through
That brutal flow of thoughts.
Our "Open" sign declared,
"Welcome!
Get out of the hot sun.
It's cool and quiet in here."

Compulsively dusted tidy shelves.
A stranger sauntered into the store.
After a furtive glance,
Bent back to my task.

"Excuse me!
Do you work here?"

What gave me away?
The garish uniform?
The cheery nametag?
The jangling keys at my waist?

"How may I help you?"

"Sharon, is that really you?"

I peered at the woman.
It was an old classmate.

"It's our 40th Reunion.
You'll be there?"

Mumbled, "Working that night."

"You own this place?
Rearrange your schedule?
Let's catch up."

"Nope, just a peon.
My regular shift.
Can't change this late."

Shocked look.
Good manners kept her quiet.
"Just need little things.
Staying with my folks."

Rang up her sale.
She swept away,
Waved good-bye,
Repeated her invitation.

Threw me off.
Curiosity was arm wrestling
With shame.
I had planned to be
Influential
Powerful
A voice for the meek.
Here I was,
Selling lottery tickets
And dried out hot dogs.

The bell chimed once more.

Would I be interrupted all day?
She had come back.

"Did you forget something?"
Had not meant to snarl,
But taming
Ferocious demons
Is taxing,
You see?

"No.
Wanted to talk to you again.
Have something to say."

Oh, boy.
A new humiliation?

"We were sophomores,
Had a short conversation.
Waiting for the bus,
I was depressed.
My story had been rejected.
School newspaper mocked it.
You knew my struggles,
Feeble hopes.
Your work was accepted,
Won prizes,
Got noticed.
Remember?"

I nodded.
Highlight of puberty
For a pale wallflower.

Made me want to
Bend time
With my words.

"You assured me
I was good.
You begged me to prevail.
You helped,
Defended,
Never asked for favors in return.
Never forgot your kindness."

I was surprised.
She was popular.
Never seemed to lack
Confidence
Or friends.

"The memory of
Your voice
And reassurance
Saved me
Many times since."

"You a writer today?"

Peals of laughter.
"Goodness, no!
Honed other, better skills.
You?"

"Nah.
Gave up the artistic life.
Costs more emotionally
Than it pays financially."

"I thought you had a rare gift.
Sorry you let it fade."

Quick hug.
Friendlier parting.
Mist of regret surrounding us both.
Damn those peeks
Into worlds that I
Would never enter.

Now had a lighter step.
Genuine smiles for my customers.
Lost track of next three hours.
Renegade musings were silent.
Calm commute.
Sang to oldies tunes.

Recalled ambitions for a Newbery Award.
Old notebooks?
Attic?
Basement trunk?

Whoa!
That old, tired master taunted again.
No enthusiasm left
For chasing fireflies
In a twilight meadow.

Mailbox held a reunion invitation.
One more chance.
Brave enough?
Could I follow a faint path
Though birds had eaten
All the markers along the way?

I dialed the unfamiliar number
Before my brain caught up
To my palpitating heart.
"Do you have room for one more?"

ABOUT THE AUTHOR

Jo-Jo Tabayoyong Murphy has another world that thrives in her imagination. She visits often! She grew up reading whatever book caught her eye as she wandered in various libraries and book stores. Deft authors taught her that words may create a universe that is as real, or surreal, as the plane on which she lives.

Jo-Jo is grateful for her husband, Steve, and daughter, Aubrey, two lights always beckoning her home.

Made in the USA
Columbia, SC
30 May 2018